Tourist Trap Murder

A Jackson Hole Moose's Bakery Not So Cozy Mystery #4

Sue Pepper

DIMICK LANE
PRESS

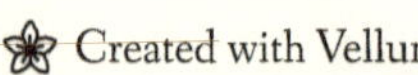 Created with Vellum

To my Dad. I carry your love and unending support and belief in me everywhere I go. Miss you.

Content Warning

Aside from the traditional off-page murder in this murder mystery, this book also contains themes of right-wing conspiracy theories, authoritarianism, and prejudice, specifically relating to the 2020 election in America.

Chapter One

"I'm not doing it, Dad. No way!" Sadie Moose turned her back resolutely on her father, Arlo, who was holding *the monstrosity* in front of him and waving it with agitation. She squeezed by Max, her head assistant baker, who was rolling out pie dough and bolted for the back of the bakery. Maybe she could hide from her dad in the walk-in.

"Sadie Louise Moose," Arlo said in the stern voice he used to use when she came home past curfew. He was right behind her again. Max must've let him by. She could hear a muffled laugh coming from their direction, and her spine stiffened. *That traitor!*

"Don't Sadie Louise Moose me, Dad," Sadie groaned, her hand on the walk-in door handle. She straightened her shoulders and turned around, crossing her arms over her chest. "I'm thirty-two years old, own a home and business, and employ a dozen people. You can't scold me like a child anymore."

The words rolled off Arlo like the sweat that was dripping off her brow. A cold sweat. A sweat that knew she would give in. That she would wear *the monstrosity*. In public. But not until she'd put up a good fight, dangit.

"I know that, dear," Arlo said. He looked around the bakery kitchen, sentiment flashing across his weathered face. When he looked back at her, his lip trembled. "You've taken over the business your mom and I built and made it something we couldn't have imagined. We're so proud of you."

Sadie barely kept herself from rolling her eyes. He was laying it on thick. Was that a tear?

"I owe you a lot, Dad," Sadie agreed, slumping against the walk-in. "But this is not how I want to repay you. Please. Anything but this."

Arlo sniffled. The gleam in his eye was definitely a tear. "It's always been my dream, you know. If you don't do this, it will be unfulfilled."

Sadie snorted. "The performance is six days a week until Labor Day. Surely Amanda will be better tomorrow."

Arlo frowned. "But today's our debut! They sidelined us all summer, but today we're back, and for the first time, Outlaw number two, Dirty Arlo, a character I've been working on for *years*, comes to life. In front of an audience. And without you... I'll miss my big chance." His voice cracked.

Sadie tilted her head and studied him. Shit. Was he acting, or was he truly upset? He wiped away a tear, *the monstrosity* swinging wildly in a flounce of ruffle and lace as he let up his grip. Sadie gulped. Fuck. She was going to give in.

"Fine, Dad," Sadie said, snatching the saloon girl gown out of his hands with a shudder. "I'll do it. But get me my lines! I won't be making a bigger fool of myself than I have to."

Arlo immediately straightened, grinning.

Ah. So it had been an act. The acting classes he'd been taking in Arizona since he'd retired had improved his skills. Sadie was grudgingly impressed.

"You'll be fantastic, dear!" He whooped at her. "And so will I, Dirty Arlo! Now, don't worry, you only have one line. It's mostly about...the look." He glanced at the dress Sadie clutched and then back at her face.

Sadie groaned. "You're telling me I have to wear this thing and I only have one line? What is it?"

Arlo shifted from foot to foot. "Uh...it's basically...help me! Please!"

Max's muffled chuckle boomed into a full laugh, and Sadie glowered at them behind her dad. "If you think this is so funny, you wear the dress, Maximus."

They grinned. "I've never been into dresses, Moose. Plus, I wouldn't fill that one out as well as you." Max was tall and slim, with black hair shaved on the sides and the top always pulled back in a short ponytail. They were Northern Arapahoe, with burnished copper skin and high cheekbones, and non-binary, using they/them pronouns.

Sadie took a deep, steadying breath and studied the dress. It was...orange satin. Not her best color or fabric. Low cut, with a corset built in that laced up the back, making it fit a variety of sizes. Thankfully, because she was at least three dress sizes bigger than Amanda. Lace flounced at the low-cut bodice and sleeves and fell in cascades on the skirt.

"I'm going to look like a sugared pumpkin," she muttered. Then she remembered the heat. It was mid-August, and it would be close to 100 degrees during the first Jackson Hole Shootout performance of the year this afternoon. She'd look like a sweaty beet red sugared pumpkin. Ugh.

"An adorable sugared pumpkin, pumpkin," Arlo said, rubbing his hands together. "I'm going to tell the rest of the players we're back on for the day. Dirty Arlo's crew rides, after all!" His voice was triumphant. "I'll send you the script. Meet us at the Playhouse at four! You'll need time for hair and makeup!" And with that, he banged out the back door of the bakery, a delighted lilt in his step, whistling the theme song to *The Good, The Bad, and The Ugly*. He was incorrigible.

"I think you'll look beautiful," Sage, her second assistant baker, said delicately from where she was loading sheet pans of sugar cookies into the ovens. Her beaded earrings clicked together as she tilted her head, looking at the dress. "It really is fine craftsmanship." Sage was a white woman in her mid-twenties with frizzy blonde curls and clear green eyes. She was a mixed media artist when she wasn't working in the bakery.

"Why would they choose orange? Who looks good in orange? Besides me, of course," Kamari Robinson, her head barista, said through the pass through, and Sadie groaned. By now everyone in the bakery dining room would know she was going to appear in the shootout.

"You'd be great in the performance," Sadie said to Kamari as she bundled the dress beneath her arm and stomped to the pass through to glare out at her customers, most of whom were snickering and pretending they hadn't been listening.

"Oh, I'm no actress," Kamari said. She eyed the dress balefully. Kamari was Black, an up-and-coming women's free skier and talented athlete. "That thing is awful." Subtlety was not one of Kamari's strong suits.

"A monstrosity," Sadie agreed, voicing her internal thought.

A chorus of disgruntled voices arose from the corner of the dining room. One particularly annoyed voice was louder than the rest. "I made it!" Sadie froze. *Shit.*

Kamari gave her a wicked grin, then turned to the dining room. "Denise! I didn't know you were a sewist! I thought you only knit."

Sadie peered around Kamari to find her table of regulars glaring at her, Denise Garza pouting. Sadie sighed. "I want to hear all about it, Denise," she said. "I'll be out in a minute."

"You're going to owe them big time," Max whispered behind her.

"She's dead," Sage agreed.

Sadie shuffled to her office to shove the dress into it, silently agreeing. Insulting the work of one of her table of regulars in front of her full bakery? Oh yes, they would exact their revenge on her. Better to get it over with sooner rather than later.

* * *

After depositing the orange eyesore in her office, Sadie stepped into the bakery dining room.

"Your Saloon Girl, everyone!" A voice boomed, and the bakery broke into whoops of laughter and applause. Sadie whipped her head around to glare at her friend Nash O'Conner, the brewmaster at the local brewery, but then turned to face the crowd and gave a small bow.

"For one night only, folks!" She said, waving her hands for them to quiet down.

"It's been too long since you were on the stage," Wendy Dawson, Sadie's onetime high school English teacher and drama advisor chirped from a nearby table. "The kids still watch your Ursula performance for a lesson in how to be a villain, you know."

Sadie felt a small glow of pride in her chest, as well as alarm. Over a decade later, and aside from solving a few murders, owning a second-generation bakery, and being an outspoken advocate for the exhausted workforce, she was still best known for her high school drama antics amongst some townspeople.

"Thanks, Wendy," Sadie said, giving her a smile. She waved at a few more friends, gave the confused tourists at the corner table a thumbs up, and then awkwardly made her way to her table of regulars.

Opal Fowler, their unofficial leader, was frowning at her, arms crossed over her chest. Opal was one of the only adults Sadie knew that was shorter than her. She was five feet tall in her sneakers, a white woman in her seventies with lots of flashy gold jewelry. Beside her were six other women. Opal had told her once that they kept their group closed at seven so they'd never face a tie vote. When Sadie had asked what they were voting on, Opal had gotten real cagey. All the town's gossip passed through them. They regularly summoned people to their table for interrogations and to call them to account for their transgressions. The City Clerk, Mrs. Wright, wouldn't even come in anymore because they were invariably mad at her for something. She called in her latte and muffin order and picked it up at the back door instead.

"You've always enjoyed the spotlight, girl," Zoey Fremont, the most plain-spoken one, grumbled. "Maybe a little too much." She was in her late fifties, a white woman who wore her gray hair in two long braids. She was on a day off from her job as a seasonal interpretive park ranger at Grand Teton National Park.

"Now, Zoey," Opal soothed, "let's give Sadie a chance to explain herself." She shifted the chair next to her out so Sadie could sit. "And apologize to Denise, of course."

Sadie stifled an inward groan and collapsed into the chair. Her foot bumped Opal's oversize Louis Vuitton bag and Sadie heard an irritated yelp. Opal coughed loudly into the elbow of her lavender designer tracksuit jacket and refused to meet Sadie's eyes. Sadie couldn't count the number of times she'd told Opal she couldn't bring her teacup poodle, Prada, into the bakery. She opened her mouth to tell her again, but Denise sighing heavily distracted her.

Denise sat across from her, digging through her always-present knitting bag and refusing to meet her eyes.

"I'm sorry for insulting your work, Denise," Sadie said. "I'd love to know more about it."

Denise shoved the bag back beneath her seat, then pushed her thick black hair, just beginning to silver, out of her eyes, finally looking at her. She was Hispanic, a plump, outspoken crafter and silent partner of the local yarn store. "It's not your color, orange," she admitted. "But it was the perfect color for my Maisie."

"Gorgeous skin, your Maisie," Chloe Fremont, Zoey's kinder, younger sister, said in her soft voice. "She was brilliant in that dress." Chloe wore her gray hair in a sleek bob and wore large, thick glasses. She was the head of the local quilt guild.

"It was a high school production of *Oklahoma!*" Lilith Dormer added, the bracelets on her wrists clacking together as she reached out an arm to pat Denise's shoulder. "You would've still been a little girl, Sadie." Lilith was white, with dark black hair in a sharp widow's peak.

Sadie felt dread in her stomach. Maisie? Denise never talked about a Maisie. She knew about her other two children. *Oh no.*

"It would've been perfect for *Oklahoma!*" Sadie conceded. "I was looking at the stitching when I took it to my office. It's truly superb. Beautiful work."

Denise sniffed. "Took me three months of hand-stitching to get the flounce just right."

"And then it must've passed into the hands of the Playhouse at some point...?"

"I suppose so," Denise said. "I'll have to tell Maisie. She'll get a kick out of it being used again."

Phew, Maisie was still with them. Thank goodness.

"Well, I'm honored to wear it, even if orange isn't my color. I apologize again."

Denise nodded at her, a small smile on her face before she grabbed her phone, presumably to text her daughter.

"Humph," Zoey grumbled. "Big mouth you have, girl."

"You know, Sadie," Opal started. Sadie froze. Here it was. Her pittance.

Opal was opening her mouth to deliver her sentence when they were interrupted by the entrance of Paige Gates-Ortiz, Sadie's best friend. Her infant daughter, Luna, was strapped to her chest in a baby carrier. Paige made a beeline to the group, her face streaked with tears.

"Paige! Are you okay?"

"No!" Paige sobbed. Sadie stood, ushering Paige into her chair, but Paige waved her off, reaching her arms around her back to unbuckle Luna, letting the carrier fall forward off her chest while she cradled the sleeping baby against her.

A general coo at Luna's adorableness, from her fine black hair that stood up straight to her chubby little ankles, hummed around the table.

Well, except for Zoey, of course. "That baby needs a hat!" Zoey frowned. "Don't babies always need hats?"

"It's a hundred degrees outside." Sadie frowned at Zoey, reaching for Luna and gently nudging Paige into the chair. Tears spilled from her eyes, but whatever was bothering her wasn't bothering Luna, who still snoozed.

"Still," Zoey glowered.

"Something to shade the face but let heat out the top of the head?" Chloe suggested.

"A visor?"

"Do they make baby visors?"

"They should."

"I could." A spark of inspiration lit Denise's eyes and she had yarn and circular needles in her hands in seconds, eyeing Luna's head critically for sizing.

Sadie bit back a laugh. They were sweet, and they meant well. She bounced gently, snuggling her goddaughter to her and barely resisting kissing her fuzzy head, giving Paige a moment to get herself together.

"I like that color, Denise," Paige said once she'd mopped her tears and taken a few deep breaths. "Luna looks beautiful in teal." Paige was white, slim, and had shoulder-length strawberry blonde hair pulled into a messy topknot.

"She'll look lovely in anything," Millie Yin, who'd apparently awoken from her snooze, soothed. Millie was Chinese and had been old since Sadie was a small child. Aside from napping, her interests included her children, grandchildren, and great-grandchildren.

"Tell us what's wrong, Paige," Gretchen Whitehouse urged. She was using her finger as a bookmark in a book with a shirtless man on the cover. Sadie resisted the urge to squint at the title. Gretchen, a white woman with brown hair, always had the best spicy book recommendations.

"It's Teton Tots, the daycare," Paige sniffled. "The new owner of the building just served them with a lease termination. They're going to have to close!"

"Oh, no!" Luna jolted, and Sadie lowered her voice, bouncing more vigorously. "That's going to affect...what, thirty families? Fifty?"

"At least," Paige wailed. "And it means I won't be able to go back to my practice unless I take her with me, I guess? But how does one do therapy with a baby in the room? A toddler?" She hiccupped another sob. "I've been on the waitlist there since before I was pregnant, and now it's being stripped away, just like that!"

"I'd better call Leanne," Lilith said, pulling her phone out and squinting at the screen, looking for her oldest granddaughter's contact information. "I wonder if she knows yet. I can take care of her youngest until we figure something else out."

"I can help, too," Chloe offered.

"We can't all become babysitters," Opal harrumphed. "I'm too damn old to be chasing after munchkins." She sat up straighter. "We just won't allow the center to close." The rest of the table of regulars sat up straight at her tone. "Who is this new owner?"

Paige made a face. "Malcolm Radcliffe. He lives in the condo next door. Apparently, the kids are too loud for his precious ears, so he's kicking them out."

Sadie gasped. "That son of a bi—" She glanced at the baby in her arms and lowered her voice, "billionaire. Son of a billionaire. How dare he!"

"He dared," Paige said sourly. "And now, as usual, the workforce will pay the price." She blanched. "I didn't even think about the campaign. I probably need to drop out! But I just won my primary! But how can I be mayor without regular childcare? I need to tell the other town council members about this. There might be something the city can do."

"We'll figure this out, Paige," Sadie said, her mind whirling with possibilities. "I promise."

"You will figure it out, Sadie," Opal said, her voice serious. "You can start by talking to Malcolm. You'll see him this afternoon anyway."

"I will?"

"He's the lead in the shootout now."

"The shootout?" Paige asked, eyeing Sadie curiously.

"Long story," Sadie said, reluctantly surrendering Luna to a persistent Lilith, who clucked over her happily. "But when did Malcolm become lead in the shootout?"

"Since he financed the restoration of the stagecoach," Denise grouched, her fingers flying as a tiny baby visor took shape on her needles. "He's a talentless hack, but apparently that matters less than his money."

"Huh," Sadie mused. "I bet Bob Foster isn't very pleased with that. He was lead for a long time. I wonder why dad hasn't mentioned it?"

Paige shrugged. "Who knows? But you'll talk to Malcolm, Sadie? Maybe he doesn't understand how big of an impact this will have on the community."

Sadie considered it. She hadn't ever had a conversation with Malcolm, but they exchanged greetings when they saw each other on the street. He'd been in town a few years, working his way up the ranks at the Playhouse and making himself known on the Jackson social scene. He didn't seem malevolent, just... not good for much. It was possible he didn't understand the severity of his actions. Maybe she could help.

"Sure, I'll speak to him," Sadie said, smiling brightly at Paige and her table of regulars. After all, what was the worst that could happen?

Chapter Two

That afternoon, Sadie reviewed the script her dad had sent her as she walked the three blocks from the bakery to the Jackson Hole Playhouse, jack-o'-lantern dress slung over her shoulder. Squinting at her phone to read in the sunshine glare and dodging tourists on the boardwalk the whole way, she still got the gist of it. It wasn't too complicated.

In the scene, two outlaws confronted each other on the blocked-off street. As they faced off, about to quick draw, a saloon girl rushed into the street, screaming that the bank coach was being robbed and someone needed to help. A stagecoach clattered into the scene, robbers clinging to the outside, and a gun battle between the now hero outlaws and the robbers lit up, with the outlaws triumphant after another stagecoach lap around the square. Then the cast passed their hats for donations and invited them to the evening Playhouse dinner and a show. She really only had one line, the rest of her stage direction being "SALOON GIRL CRIES OUT" and "SALOON GIRL WAILS, BOSOM HEAVING." *Sigh.*

Arlo and Malcolm were the two outlaws, with Malcolm as lead having the final big moment, bursting out of the stagecoach, alive, after they had convinced the crowd that he had fallen off the roof to his death. It was quite a stunt. Maybe Malcolm was more talented than people gave him credit for.

She was swiping the email closed, thinking about the families that the daycare's closure would affect when she ran into a solid object and stumbled, orange satin and lace ruffles flying over her head from the impact.

"Woah there," an amused voice said, firm hands steadying her shoulders before she could fall. "Is that Sadie Moose under there?"

Sadie groaned inwardly. She knew that voice. Gasping for air, she pulled layers of satin off her face, eventually emerging red faced to frown at Detective Will Nolan.

"I should cite you for walking under the in-flounce." He reached up to pull an errant piece of lace out of her hair, his mouth crooked in amusement.

"Har har," Sadie mumbled, brushing his hand away and shaking the dress out before putting it back over her shoulder.

"Really? I thought that was a pretty good one." Will was a white man around forty, tall and lean, with interesting features that were handsome when he smiled, which he was doing now. He was clean shaven, with blonde hair and piercing blue eyes.

Sadie sighed. "It was pretty good, actually. I'm just in a bad mood. I'm sorry."

Will tilted his head. "What's up?"

Sadie glanced at her watch. It was just after four. She was running late. "Walk with me?" She gestured towards the Playhouse, still a block away.

Will shrugged. "Sure. I'm off duty. I'm headed to pick up Jaden at day camp at the park." He gestured in the same direction, and they both started walking that way.

"Does Jaden like camp?"

"Yesterday they played with paint-filled water balloons and

he came home looking like he'd bathed in a rainbow, and today they were going whitewater rafting, so yeah. He likes it fine."

Sadie chuckled. "Camp sounds way more fun than when I was a kid."

"He's seven. Almost everything's fun."

They dodged a group of tourists standing on the sidewalk taking photos with a family of chainsaw bear statues and were quiet for a moment.

"Did you hear Malcolm Radcliffe bought the Teton Tots building and is closing it?" Sadie asked suddenly.

"Yikes. No. That's terrible."

"It is. Paige is really upset. She's going to see if there's something the council can do, but I'm going to talk to Malcolm too."

"Maybe he just needs some sense talked into him," Will agreed. "But I'm less interested in that, and more interested in why you're walking around with that dress."

"What dress?" Sadie deadpanned.

"The dress I know Amanda Lyle has been wearing in rehearsals for the shootout that's premiering for the summer this afternoon."

"Well, Amanda's sick. And apparently I'm the only person who can fill in for her according to my dad, so..."

Will grinned. "I told Jaden we wouldn't do the shootout tonight, that we'd wait a few days to let everyone get the kinks out of the production, but now..."

Sadie stopped in front of the Playhouse. "I guess I'll see you there, then."

"I wouldn't miss it. Your dad's in the production?"

"Yeah. Him and Mom are back for the summer." Perhaps for good. They couldn't decide what they wanted to do. They'd retired to Arizona, but Arlo complained it was too hot and Robin complained Arlo didn't have enough to do so she couldn't even day drink with her girlfriends. "They're staying in my rental since the O'Donnells moved out." The house across the alley from her had once belonged to Merritt West, her childhood best friend and probable love of her life, but he'd signed the deed over to her last fall to give her more power over a potential housing development going in on their block. Instead of dealing with it, though, Sadie had rented it out continuously since then. Someday she'd figure it out.

"That's nice."

They looked at each other for a minute, then Sadie glanced away, feeling awkward. "I still owe you that dinner, you know."

"That you do." Last spring, Will had played a big part in getting her and others rescued off the side of a mountain while a killer was on the loose. The least Sadie owed him was dinner. "Jaden's here for another week before he goes back to his mom's, but after that?"

Sadie was opening her mouth to confirm when the Playhouse door opened and Arlo appeared, a fake mustache already applied. "Sadie! You're late! Come inside!" He looked at Will. "Detective." He tipped his nonexistent hat, then pulled Sadie through the door. She waved at Will, and he winked at her. Yeah. In a week, she'd let him take her out.

* * *

As soon as they shoehorned her into the dress, Sadie understood why she alone could pull off this role.

Her fabulous rack.

Sadie glared at the cleavage exposed in the dress. Wasn't this supposed to be a family friendly show? And really, her dad was the one that volunteered her? Ugh.

"You look fab, Sadie," Juliana Galvan, the Playhouse costumer and hair and makeup artist enthused from her position on the floor, using a handheld steamer to get wrinkles out of the satin. She was a curvy white woman in her twenties with a trendy dark bob and square glasses. She was an in-demand hairstylist at one of the fancier salons in town, too.

"Is there supposed to be this much boob?"

"Yep." Juliana stood and adjusted the lace on the neckline, stepping back to eye her critically. Sadie's brown hair was piled on top of her head and adorned with a rhinestone-and-feather headpiece that gave her an extra foot of height. Her pale cheeks were rouged, her lips painted red, false eyelashes applied, along with heavy eye makeup that enhanced her green eyes. "Honestly, you look better than Amanda," she said conspiratorially.

"Don't tell Amanda that," a voice boomed from behind them, and Sadie turned to see Malcolm Radcliffe there, resplendent in his wild west gunfighter costume. Malcolm was of average height, a white man with thinning dark hair and a ruddy complexion.

Juliana rolled her eyes at Sadie, then turned to Malcolm, smiling brightly. "Of course I wouldn't, sir."

He ignored her, moving forward to eye Sadie. "You look passable, though, really. Thank you for filling in on such short notice. And you've read the script?"

"I've memorized all one of my lines," Sadie said dryly, clenching her teeth at being called merely "passable".

"And you think you can keep up with the choreography?" Malcolm pulled a vape pen out of the inside pocket of his duster and sucked in deeply.

"Wailing and throwing myself about? Absolutely."

"Excellent," Malcolm said, not picking up on her sarcasm, taking another hit off his pen. "Just follow my lead if you get confused."

"Thanks," Sadie said, but Malcolm was already walking away, bumping into the doorway on his way through.

"Asshole," Juliana muttered under her breath, and Sadie

snorted. "But I hope whatever Amanda has isn't going around." She lowered her voice. "I had to put on twice as much blush as usual to give him some color today. He was pale as a sheet when he came in."

"Huh," Sadie said. "He shouldn't be performing if he's sick."

"You couldn't pull this opening day away from his cold, dead hands," Juliana laughed. "They've all worked too hard for this, and Malcolm, well, he doesn't work very hard, but he's spent a lot of money."

"I'm glad I could step in so it could continue," Sadie said, confident finally in her role. She did look fantastic, even in orange, and she could roll with this. She was saving the day. Saloon-girl-Sadie to the rescue!

"Time to go, players!" Arlo's voice rang out from the stage, and Sadie took a deep breath. Or she attempted to. The corset was so tight, she couldn't quite manage it. So she took a few quick breaths instead. In an hour, this would all be over.

It was on the walk to the town square when Sadie finally started feeling it.

The thrill of being on stage.

The unfurling of a character inside of her, taking over her movements, her smiles.

The rising adrenaline of performing in front of a group.

And the nerves. Of going on stage without ever rehearsing. The stuff of her actual nightmares. She ran through the script in her head again and again. She could do this.

They caused a stir on their way, which was the point of the walk. Tourists with their interest piqued followed them as they waltzed down the street. There were seven of them total. Arlo, Malcolm, Sadie, the stagecoach driver, and the three actors playing stagecoach robbers. The only one Sadie knew was Cody Carter, the stagecoach driver, who was a rodeo clown and bull-fighter in the twice-weekly summer rodeo and a frequent customer: black coffee and a vegan blueberry muffin.

When they neared the streets surrounding the town square, Sadie saw the crowd. Playhouse workers had put up the temporary roadblocks to reroute traffic. She saw flashing police lights and glimpsed Officer Greg Knott's buzz cut through the crowd as he routed vehicles off the main road and onto a side street. The shootout was a big deal. They had canceled it during the pandemic, then it had been plagued by staffing and equipment troubles, and the city had considered canceling it altogether. But with an influx of cash from Malcolm and pressure from the businesses on the town square that counted on the daily summer attraction to pull tourists into their t-shirt and souvenir and ice cream shops, the Playhouse had pulled together a show for the first time in three years, and town was turning out for it.

Malcolm pulled them into an alley for a quick pre-production pep talk, a bottle of acid reducers in hand. He shook a few out and chomped them before slipping the bottle back into his coat pocket and pulling his vape pen out. His neck was flushed under his collar and bolo tie and sweat beaded at his brow, furrows of it cutting through the makeup caked on his face. Sadie wondered if he was too hot. She certainly was.

"We've been practicing all summer for this!" Malcolm coughed into his elbow once, then twice, before taking a rattly breath. The man did *not* seem well, but the show was going on, regardless.

Malcolm continued his pep talk. "Arlo, remember to be mean."

Arlo snarled and twirled his mustache. "I'm your huckleberry," he growled.

Sadie snickered, then sobered when Malcolm glared at her.

"You know your line?"

"Yes, sir," Sadie said. He continued to glare, and Sadie rolled her eyes, then fell into character. "Please, somebody, help me. The bank stage is being robbed!" She wailed, staggering, bosom heaving.

"That'll do," Malcolm sighed. "Cody, you better get the coach. We're on in five."

"Break a leg, kid," Arlo said gleefully, pulling Sadie into a hug. "Thanks for doing this."

"You bet, Dad," Sadie said, giving him a squeeze back.

"Places!" Malcolm called, and they broke up, slipping out of the alley and dissolving into the crowd that surrounded the blocked-off street. From there, Arlo and Malcolm would square off, Sadie would blend into the crowd to make her entrance, and Cody and the robbers would go to their staging area a block away, ready to squeal onto the scene.

Sadie took a deep breath. Well, a short, panting breath thanks to the corset. She dug into the hidden pocket of the dress for a handkerchief and pressed it to her sweaty brow. She was excited to be out of the dress, to have the scene over with...but in the meantime, she'd allow herself to have some fun.

Chapter Three

Blending into the crowd was tough when you shone like a mountain sunset and half of everyone you'd ever known had shown up to see your performance. In between hellos and waves, Sadie wound her way through the crowd to her designated place, only to find it occupied by her entire staff, who greeted her with whoops and hollers.

"I'm supposed to be blending in," Sadie hissed, stepping into their circle.

"I'll hide you," Kendall Craig, her business partner, assured her, stepping in front of her and puffing herself up to look intimidating. Sadie rolled her eyes. Kendall, a white woman with close cropped dark hair and delicate piercings along her ears, was a whole inch taller than her and about half her size.

"No, I've got this," Jorge Garcia, her day manager who was roughly the size of a mountain, sighed, hip checking Kendall out of the way. Jorge was Hispanic, a retired high school football coach. His grandkids, Miles and Hazel, sat on his shoulders, and Sadie stuck her tongue out at them when they made faces at her. She was blending in, alright.

"Are you nervous?" Sage asked, worry in her tone. "I'm

always nervous before shows." She occasionally did performance art, as well as her mixed media work. Max patted Sage's arm.

"Sadie's an old pro at this," they assured her.

"You look lovely," a voice said from behind her, and she turned to see her mom, Robin, grinning at her. She was a white woman in a golf visor, her graying hair pulled back in a stubby ponytail. "I told Arlo you looked great in orange."

"You're such a liar," Sadie laughed. The surrounding crowd quieted and Sadie glanced around the Jorge-and-grandkids mountain to her makeshift stage. Arlo and Malcolm had stepped onto the road. She had about five minutes.

The two men immediately commanded attention as they aired their grievances with one another, each more ridiculous than the last. Arlo was the picture of an outlaw, all bluster and fancy tricks. He drew laughter more than once. Malcolm was less talented, somehow too melodramatic for an old west shootout that called for melodramatics. As the two worked each other up to where they were about to quick draw, Sadie noticed Malcolm stumble once, and she held her breath. Had he tripped? Was he okay? But he quickly recovered.

And then it was her turn.

Drawing the deepest breath she could, she screamed once, twice, then stumbled out onto the street, rushing between the two men as they were about to shoot.

"Help, please!" Sadie wailed, stumbling on her feet. "The bank stage! It's being robbed!"

The crowd gasped as she fainted, Arlo catching her before she could fall to the ground. The stagecoach, led by a matched pair of Clydesdales, rolled onto the scene, robbers hooting and hollering from the sides and where they held Cody hostage.

"Good job," Arlo whispered to Sadie as he lowered her to the ground, where she was supposed to faint for a few minutes.

Then he rushed off to engage in the battle with the coach robbers.

The pavement was hot and sweat trickled down her back, but she managed to lay still until her next cue, when she hopped up to observe the fight. The stage direction here was to improvise if the crowd was into it, and she could see that the crowd was *definitely* into it. Spying Jaden Nolan nearby wearing a Pikachu backpack, she sidled up to him and asked if she could borrow it, then snuck up behind a robber that was about to take out Arlo, feigning hitting him over the head with it. The crowd erupted in laughter as he fell to the ground, moaning, and cheered for Jaden as she tossed it back to him. Sadie watched the robber, but he winked at her. Apparently, he was out for the count.

The scene was winding towards its conclusion, with two robbers laid out on the pavement, the other battling Arlo and Malcolm. The outlaws cornered the robber against the stagecoach, but instead of giving in, he leapt onto the stagecoach step, roaring for Cody to step on it or die as he brandished an old-timey pistol. Arlo and Malcolm grabbed onto the stage before it could roll away and thus began the most dangerous part of the act. Sadie knew they'd been practicing this for weeks. Atop the stagecoach, the three would battle as it went around the town square. By the time it came back into the square, Arlo would've fallen to his death, as well as the other robber, and then Malcolm would emerge triumphant from the coach as it rolled back onto the scene, clutching bags with dollar signs printed on them for the crowd to fill with tips before they all took their bows.

Sadie watched with the audience, heaving her bosom dramatically and crying out as appropriate. When Arlo fell off the stage, her breath really did hitch, but she knew he had climbed down the side they couldn't see and was winding his way through the town square park towards her. Then the second outlaw fell, and then Malcolm, and the crowd was in near hysterics as the stagecoach pulled back in. Had it all been for not? Had both outlaws died?

Sadie held her breath as she waited for the stagecoach door to open.

Her eyes flicked to Cody, who frowned back at her.

A horse nickered.

It was quiet. The crowd was silent, waiting.

Had something gone wrong? Malcolm was pushing the crowd's patience. He should've been out already.

Arlo appeared behind the stagecoach and frowned at Sadie, who gave a small shrug. He was supposed to be dead. Time for some improv.

"Did no one survive?" Sadie wailed, careening towards the coach. "My dearest Outlaw," she cried, holding her arms out towards the door. "Please tell me you're alive!"

Cody raised an eyebrow at her. But so what? She was inventing a love story between Malcolm and the saloon girl. Why not? Wasn't the first rule of improv always answering with, "yes, and..."?

Still no answer from inside the coach.

"Open the door," Arlo hissed from where he was hiding. The crowd was getting restless. Sadie felt uneasy.

"I'll rescue you, my darling," Sadie boomed, reaching for the door, hoping it would open before she could do so.

Her hand grasped the handle.

It turned.

The door swung open.

And she screamed before crumpling to the ground.

* * *

Sadie prided herself on having never fainted in her life. She wasn't the sort to take any news without aplomb. She was made of sturdy stuff, a Wyoming girl who could ski the toughest terrain, ride a horse when pressed to do so, navigate a raft through rapids, and run a growing company with over a dozen employees. She'd even found a few dead bodies before and had never fainted.

So later, once she'd woken up on the pavement with the worried faces of her staff and mom leaning over her, a misting fan borrowed from a tourist trained on her face, she blamed it solely on the corset. The constriction on her rib cage, the way she couldn't get a full breath, the terrible heat...that was the reason she'd fainted dead away.

Not that she'd found Malcolm Radcliffe dead in the stagecoach.

Things were a blur from that moment on. Eventually, they moved her into a nearby air-conditioned t-shirt shop to cool down, the sign flipped to closed behind them. Robin loosened the corset to Sadie's great relief. Sirens wailed outside. An ambulance was ushered onto the street. The crowd was both trying to disperse and trying to watch, and the police that had been doing traffic control were doing their best to keep people back and move them along.

"Where's Dad?" Sadie asked once she'd taken a sip of water and insisted on being allowed to sit up.

Robin bit her lip and glanced outside. She had taken off her visor and was turning it in her hands nervously.

"Your dad stepped in to do CPR," Kendall said. "He's a hero."

"CPR? But he was...dead dead right?"

"I thought so," Kendall shrugged. "Either way, him and the other robbers got him out of the coach and started doing CPR.

Will jumped in, too. Now the paramedics have taken over, so maybe he's not dead dead."

Will. Right. He'd been there with Jaden. Where was Jaden?

Sadie focused in on Kamari. "Can you see if Will needs us to look after Jaden? They were watching the shootout."

"On it," Kamari said, and disappeared out the door.

"Huh," Max said, gawking out the window.

"What?"

"The paramedics loaded him up with a thing on his face. Guess he's not dead dead."

"What did you see when you looked in the stagecoach?" Robin asked. "No one could see around you, and once you fainted, I didn't look in."

Sadie shuddered. "Malcolm was on the floor of the coach. His face was red and swollen, and his...tongue was hanging out of his mouth. Like he'd suffocated? It must've been a terrible accident. Or maybe a heart attack? It had to have happened so quickly!"

"Malcolm wasn't steady on his feet throughout the performance," Kendall said. "Maybe he wasn't feeling well." Sadie had noticed him stumble more than once, too, and Juliana had said he needed extra makeup to get color in his cheeks. Maybe he'd succumbed to an illness.

"He was a no-talent over actor," a voice grumbled behind her, and Sadie turned in shock. It was Ted Schultz, the owner of Schultz's Shirts. Ted was a white man in his fifties with a buzz cut and a beer belly.

"That's a little harsh, considering what just happened," Robin admonished.

Ted adjusted the red hat on his head. "I said what I said. We've wanted the shootout back for years, and now look how he mucked it up on opening day!"

"By probably dying?" Sadie blinked.

"Overacting, then probably dying. I'm not even getting any business out of this! I should be selling t-shirts right now, not sheltering you."

"I'm happy to leave if you'd like, Ted," Sadie groaned, getting to her feet. "You can open up and sell your shirts."

"You've always been an asshole," Kendall said to Ted as the group moved towards the door. "Don't think I don't know about your opposition to the Pride Parade."

Ted's face flushed as red as his hateful hat. "I'm allowed to have my opinions."

"Your opinions are shit," Max said.

"Thanks for the cool air," Robin said loudly, and pulled the group out onto the boardwalk. Kamari was on her way in, Jaden in tow. One look at the wide-eyed boy, the curious crowd, and the ambulance starting to pull away, and Sadie decided.

"To the bakery," she said. "We all deserve cookies."

Chapter Four

A sheet tray of decorated sugar cookies on the table between them, Sadie huddled with her crew in her now-closed bakery. She'd changed out of the wretched dress into a Moose's Bakery t-shirt and the pair of leggings she kept in her office for batter-and-flour emergencies. The air conditioning was cranked and Kamari was force-feeding her a second bottle of water. Jorge and his grandkids had taken their cookies to go, so it was Sadie, Kamari, Kendall, Robin, Max, Sage, and Jaden.

After stuffing his mouth with two cookies in rapid succession, Jaden dug into his backpack for his tablet and headphones, then set up at a table by the window, another cookie in front of him.

"Hey Jaden, is that Pikachu?" Kendall said loudly, pointing out the window.

Jaden didn't move.

"Perfect," she said, clapping her hands together. "Little ears can't hear us, so dish. What the hell just happened?"

"Your guess is as good as mine," Sadie said, pushing away

the third bottle of water Kamari was holding out to her. Her stomach felt sloshy and ill.

"How old is Malcom?" Robin asked.

"Late thirties?" Sadie guessed.

"Too young for a heart attack, right?" Max had an arm around Sage, who looked near tears. Sage was a sensitive soul.

"Not necessarily," Kamari said.

"Maybe the stunt went wrong, and he injured himself that way?" Robin got up to peer out the window, looking for Arlo.

"It seemed like it went fine to me," Sadie mused. She shuddered, trying to get the image of Malcolm's red face out of her head. "But that could have happened. How terrible."

There were murmurs of agreement all around.

"But at least Teton Tots most likely won't close now," Kendall said, ever the optimist.

"He's not dead yet, Kendall!" Sadie scolded.

"But maybe?"

"There is that," Sadie allowed. "But I bet this is the end of the shootout, no matter what happens."

"Seems antiquated anyway," Max said. They stood from their chair. "Everyone done with cookies?" When everyone nodded, they took the tray through the door to the kitchen.

"That's what people like about it, is that it's an old-time thing," Robin protested, sitting back down.

"True, but it does seem a little irresponsible, honestly, with the gun problem this country has." Sadie agreed with Max. But the tourist trap it created was essential to the businesses on the town square, like Schultz's Shirts.

"Well, they won't have to worry about it anymore," said a new voice at the door, and Robin jumped up as Arlo pushed his way in miserably. His villainous mustache was half off his face, fluttering in the air conditioning breeze. He'd pulled off his duster and Sadie thought he looked small without it, shoulders slumped.

"Oh Dad, come in," Sadie said, rushing to his side with her mother. "Sit down, let us get you some water."

They bustled about, getting Arlo settled into a chair with a plate of cookies and water, then all gathered about again, watching him expectantly.

"What happened to Malcolm?" Sadie asked when she couldn't wait any longer.

"I don't know," Arlo said after gulping water. "The police said there weren't signs of the stunt going wrong, at least."

"That's good."

"It's awful," Arlo moaned.

"Did the paramedics actually think he would make it?"

"Hard to tell."

"We can hope and pray that he does," Robin said, looking at the group with censure. "Despite if he was a nice man or not, he doesn't deserve to die."

"Well, he killed the shootout. Probably for good," Arlo bemoaned, ripping his fake mustache off so he could shove a cookie in his mouth. Robin patted his shoulder.

Her phone vibrated in her pocket, and she pulled it out. Will.

"Hey, Will. Jaden's still here at the bakery with me."

"Thanks for taking him." Will sounded weary. "I'm going to be late. Can you keep him for a bit? I can try calling my regular babysitter—"

"He can hang with us, no problem," Sadie interrupted. "We're going to head to my house soon. We'll order pizza for dinner. Does he have any allergies?"

"No, but his mom doesn't like him having too much sugar." Sadie winced at the pile of crumbs in front of Jaden and the icing smeared across his face. Welp. Too late. "—but I don't care about the sugar," Will continued, and that made her feel a little better.

"Okay," Sadie said. "Text me when you think you can come get him. We'll put on a movie. He can fall asleep on the couch if he gets sleepy."

"You're a lifesaver, Sadie. This is a mess."

He'd piqued her interest, but she tamped it down. She could ask later. "No problem. Want to talk to Jaden for a minute?"

Will wanted to, so Sadie got Jaden's attention and handed the phone to him before turning back to her crew. "Time to disperse, friends."

Robin and Arlo stood. "Call us if you need help with the little man," Robin said.

Sadie hugged her dad. "I'm sorry about all this."

"No, I'm sorry," he said, squeezing her tight. "I got you involved, and you had to be the one to find him."

"I'll be fine," she said. She wrinkled her nose. "You stink, Dirty Arlo. Go shower."

"Shower beer, Arlo!" Kendall said. "You deserve a shower beer!"

Max and Sage were the next to leave. The two had become fast friends over the last months, and Sadie had wondered more than once if they were romantically involved. They were private people, though, so Sadie hadn't pried.

"See you in the morning," Sadie called as they left through the kitchen door.

Then it was just her, Kendall, Kamari, and Jaden, who had hung up with his dad and was packing his tablet into his backpack.

"We get to order pizza? Cool!"

"My dude, we are going to order so much pizza," Kendall said. "Walk with me? I need to know your opinion. Who's more powerful, Squirtle or Bulbasaur?"

Jaden's eyes lit up as he walked through the door, and Sadie could hear him chattering away at Kendall over the varied powers of the two Pokémon as they headed towards Sadie's house.

"I'll lock up, Moose," Kamari said from beside her. "You head home with them."

"I can't help but feel this isn't over," Sadie said, and Kamari put a gentle hand on her shoulder.

"It probably isn't. Malcom is trouble."

Sadie sighed.

"But we'll face it together, Moose, whatever happens."

Sadie hugged Kamari, then walked out the door, out into the August heat that felt like one of the pizza ovens at Slice Slice Baby, which she called as she started home.

"Yeah, Augustine? We're going to need some pizza. Lots of pizza."

* * *

It was a good thing Sadie didn't cook much because they had a lot of leftovers.

Even with the entire bakery crew showing back up throughout the evening to entertain Jaden, gab about the day's events, and devour slices, Sadie still shoved four boxes into her fridge.

"Good thing I moved out, huh?" Gavin Vincent, her new-to-town chef friend said as he leaned against her counter, a slice of mushroom and arugula pizza in his hand, echoing her thoughts. Gavin was a white man with dark hair, a perpetually stubbled square jaw, steely gray eyes, and a variety of food-related tattoos. He'd stayed with her over the summer until finding his own place near the restaurant he'd bought.

Sadie wrinkled her nose, remembering the fridge full of

carefully labeled plastic prep containers he hadn't allowed her to touch. "I'd never seen my fridge so full. So organized. So off limits."

"One does not mess with my creations," Gavin agreed.

Sadie had eaten well while he'd been her roommate, though she had grown weary of waiting for him to plate things with his tweezers and take a picture before serving it to her.

"Well, Jaden's out," Kamari said, coming into the kitchen with a pile of paper plates and depositing them in the trash.

"Good," Sadie said. She glanced at her watch. It was almost ten. Who knew how long it would be before Will could make it back to pick him up. The longer he was gone, the more Sadie worried over what he could be investigating. Would this much time need to go into a simple natural death investigation? "Thank you for helping with him."

"He's a good kid," Kamari yawned. "I'm heading to bed." She waved as she left out the back door, aiming for her basement apartment entrance. Kamari shared the apartment with Sage, but Sage had started spending fewer and fewer nights there. Was she with Max? Kamari was never worried, so Sadie tried not to worry about her, too.

"Night, Kamari," Sadie said, suppressing a yawn herself.

"What are you going to do with the kid if he's here all night?" Gavin asked, brushing his hands off on a napkin and swigging from the can of IPA he held.

Sadie shrugged. "Sleep on the other couch, I guess."

"Good thing I made you get new ones," Gavin said smugly. He crumpled the can into a perfect puck in a move Sadie couldn't quite follow, tossed it in the recycling, and kissed her on the forehead. "I'm headed out, too."

She said goodbye while frowning at him. Sadie had recently sold the old leather couches she'd inherited from her parents when she bought their house from them at Gavin's insistence, only to have Kendall and Kamari end up buying them for their living rooms. She'd replaced them with reasonable adult grownup mid-century modern pieces, and she hated them with every ounce of her being. They were stiff and uncomfortable. Every time she sat on one, she realized she'd gone a step too far in making her former childhood home her now adult home. She gazed around the kitchen decorated with red apples, from the apple clock on the wall to the apple knobs on the cabinets. She'd planned on redoing this room, too, but after the couch mistake she'd backed out. It was kitschy and outdated, and she loved it. So there.

A buzz of her phone interrupted her, and she looked at it to see a notification for motion at her front door. She squinted at the picture. Will.

Stepping quickly but quietly to intercept him at the door before he could knock and wake up her chocolate Labrador Retriever, Tyrone, she walked to the front door, peering in at Jaden on the way to make sure he was still sleeping. A cartoon played in the dark room, casting shadows on his face. Tyrone was curled up on the floor next to him, snoring lightly, head resting on Jaden's backpack. She made it to the door just before Will could knock. He looked weary.

"Mind the doormat," she chided, gesturing. He glanced at it and laughed.

"Please text, there's no need to get the dog involved," he read. "I'd forgotten."

"You're tired," she said in a soft voice. He looked rumpled and exhausted, bags under his brilliant blue eyes.

"I am," he said in the same tone. "Jaden asleep?"

"Yep, passed out cold despite the sugar cookies and soda I fed him between bites of pizza."

He smiled weakly. "I can take him home."

Sadie studied him. "Have you eaten? I have more leftover pizza than I could eat in a week."

"As long as this doesn't count as that date you promised me, I'd love some pizza. And a beer?"

"A dinner is not automatically a date," Sadie said, opening the door and gesturing him inside. "Especially a thank you dinner."

"Hmm," he said, peering into the living room at Jaden, a smile on his face.

Sadie waved him into the kitchen and he followed, taking a seat at her counter and rubbing his eyes.

"Cold pizza or microwaved?"

"Cold is fine."

Sadie plated him an assortment of slices and put them in front of him, then grabbed them both a beer and sat next to him.

He ate in silence for a minute, and Sadie took a drink of her beer. It was a crisp summer ale by the local brewery, a seasonal favorite she wouldn't be able to enjoy much longer. It may have been the middle of August, but that meant the weather would change soon. They usually saw snow in the valley by Halloween.

"Honestly, your restraint is impressive," Will said finally, breaking the silence. He cracked open his beer and took a drink.

Sadie blinked. "Oh?"

"I thought you'd be asking me about the case immediately."

Sadie blanched. "Ugh, if it's a case that means it's more than just an accident, doesn't it?"

"You know it."

"Okay, fine. I'll bite. Is Malcolm alive?"

"No. They pronounced him dead at the hospital."

"Shit."

"Mmmhmm."

"And you have reason to believe it wasn't an accident?"

Will took another drink of his beer, thinking. "Am I drinking a beer in your house?"

"Yes...?"

"That means I'm off duty, right?"

"I would think so."

"Okay. Then I'm going to tell you something, and you didn't hear it from me."

Sadie could barely contain her shock. Detective Will Nolan, divulging case information to her? How far they'd come since he'd thought her the number one suspect in the murder of her nemesis last fall.

Will finished his last piece of pizza and wiped his mouth with a napkin while Sadie waited impatiently.

"Call Mateo," he said finally, and Sadie gasped. Mateo was Paige's husband. And Sadie's lawyer.

"You don't think I had something to do with this!" she squeaked, standing abruptly.

"No, I don't. But preliminary testing shows that Malcolm might have been poisoned."

Sadie gasped again.

"And right now, the last person to see him alive was your dad."

"You can't possibly think my dad killed him!"

"We've been over this before. It doesn't matter much what I think, it matters what the evidence says. Call Mateo in the morning. Get your dad a lawyer. And I didn't say that to you."

He stood. "Thank you for taking care of Jaden for me."

"This is the worst date I've ever been on," Sadie hissed at him as he walked out of the kitchen to collect Jaden.

"Not a date," Will said.

"You're right. People that accuse my father of murder don't get dates with me."

A muscle in Will's jaw clenched, and he took a step towards

her. Her back was against the wall suddenly, and she was reminded how much taller he was than her, how bright and direct his blue eyes were, how even after a long day of work he smelled faintly of aftershave and the nicotine gum she saw him chew now and then.

"Sadie Moose," he said, his voice low, firm. "When I take you on a date, you will know it. This was not a date."

"You're not taking me on one," she said, a pouty note in her voice. Where had that come from? Sadie squared her shoulders and pushed off the wall. "Now you and Jaden need to leave."

"The least you could say is thanks for the heads up," he said in a low voice near her ear, and Sadie stepped away to hide her shiver. Damn the man for being sexy as hell. Damn her for owing him a favor. Damn *him* for accusing her father of murder!

"Fine," she said through gritted teeth. "I appreciate the heads up. No one in my family will have a comment without a lawyer present as a heads up to you."

"I'd expect nothing less." Will stepped away from her and to the couch, where he scooped Jaden up into his arms. Sadie handed him Jaden's backpack, which he slung over a shoulder, the kid-size backpack very small against his broad back. She held the door open for him, and he stepped through it.

"Good night, Sadie," he said wryly. "We can fight more tomorrow."

Sadie sighed. "Good night, Will." And she shut the door.

Chapter Five

Sadie was in high school the first time the developers came for Moose's. She'd been a sophomore, a plump sixteen-year-old with a shiny new driver's license and a shinier complexion. She'd been auditioning for the high school production of Annie and spent her early mornings mixing doughs alongside Arlo, singing the songs in harmony.

Then, one morning, he hadn't been singing anymore. His face had been grim as he laminated pastry dough with more force than necessary. Sadie had spent the school day worrying he was dying until that night at dinner he'd explained that the bakery's landlord was considering taking an offer for the block from a luxury hotel developer.

The look on Arlo's face had been unlike one Sadie had ever seen. She'd never seen him look defeated unless he was acting. But this hadn't been a production. This was their livelihood, the dream of her parents, the love story they'd built together in the cabin that always smelled of sugar cookies. Fueled by teenage-hormone-induced-rage and the sheer audacity of out-of-towners, Sadie had insisted they could and would fight it.

Sitting across from her at the kitchen table, Sadie's parents had studied her, and perhaps because her ears were pink, which meant she was really mad, or perhaps because they were well acquainted with a teenage girl's temper, they didn't argue. They asked her what they should do. They brought her into the running of the bakery in a way that meant more than knowing the secret recipes, and there, plates pushed aside and notebook and freshly sharpened Dixon Ticonderoga #2 pencils in hand, they plotted their plan to save the bakery.

It had worked.

And now, sitting across from her parents at the same kitchen table, just with her at the head of it instead of her father, Sadie remembered their playbook for that fight, the one they'd put back into play every time the developers threatened the bakery. She could use it again to defend her dad. She could use it, and her investigation skills she'd honed in the last year, to save him from scrutiny. It was on her now.

"For the love, Sadie Louise, you're giving me a stress headache just looking at you," Robin said finally, taking a sip of her tea.

"Just spit it out, girl," Arlo agreed, stirring creamer into his coffee. "We're not fragile, you know."

Sadie took a deep breath. She'd let her parents get a good night's rest, then asked them over for coffee before she needed to be at the bakery. Arlo was dressed for his morning run, including a reflective vest and bear spray attached to his waistband. The vest kept catching the light and half blinding her. Robin was dressed for golf.

"Listen, Will came over last night—"

"Oooh," Robin said, putting her tea down and leaning in. "He did?"

"To pick up Jaden," Sadie said with emphasis.

"Right, right," Robin said, remembering. "*Right.*" She looked nervous suddenly and glanced at Arlo.

"And he said—"

"That Malcolm was dead and probably murdered by poison?" Arlo broke in, then took a sip of coffee nonchalantly.

Sadie gaped at her dad. She checked her watch. It was six-thirty in the morning. How had he possibly found out?

"The theater," Arlo said, reading her expression. "Juliana's second cousin told her, she told Amanda, Amanda told Cody, Cody told me."

"How did Juliana's second cousin find out?"

Arlo mimed locking his lips with a key and throwing it away.

"Best not to ask, dear," Robin said, finishing her tea. "Now, if that's all you had to tell us, I think I'll be off. Early tee time, you know."

"Are you not even a little worried?" Sadie cried. "You were the last person to see him alive, dad!"

Arlo shrugged. "I'm not worried because I know I had nothing to do with it."

Sadie buried her head in her hands. She'd gotten almost no sleep worrying about breaking this news to her parents, had gone over and over in her head how she would reassure them that she would protect Arlo from the investigation, how she'd poke around to figure out the real killer for him, and he was...unbothered.

"Regardless of that, you need a lawyer. I already called Mateo last night. He wants you to go by his office this morning."

"I have plans all morning."

"As long as you plan to remain not arrested, I need you go to by his office this morning."

Arlo sighed but agreed. "Fine, fine. If it'll make you feel better."

"It will," Sadie said with relief. "And don't talk to any cops without him there."

"I don't make a habit of talking to cops," Arlo assured her, standing to put his coffee cup in the dishwasher before brushing kisses over her and her mom's foreheads. "And I'm off!"

As he banged out the back door, Tyrone trotting beside him on his leash wearing his own reflective vest, Sadie blew out a deep breath. Robin reached out and patted her hand. "When you get older, it's hard to get as worried about things," she said. "You'll see. It's hard to be outraged at our ages."

* * *

"I'm outraged!" Opal screeched. A chorus of agreements echoed around the table.

Harder to be outraged when you get older, huh Mom? My table of regulars would disagree.

Sadie took a deep, calming breath. She held up her hands for quiet and gradually, the table quieted down. She studied the lined, angry faces. Lilith's normally smooth hair was messy around her head, like she'd been clutching at it. Denise had thrown down her knitting—Sadie was pretty sure it was yet another baby visor—in disgust. Gretchen had marked her paperback by dog-earing the page, something she'd surely regret later. Even Chloe was gnashing her teeth while Zoey whispered fervently into her ear. The only calm one was Millie, because she was, as usual, asleep. Beatrice Meyer, known as Ms. B, a new—non-voting—member of the group since Sadie had met her at an ill-fated mountain retreat last spring, seemed unbothered, too, but that was Ms. B. She would be stoic in the face of the apocalypse.

"Listen, I will talk to Max. It was an honest mistake."

Zoey scoffed, pushing her plate towards Sadie and jabbing a finger at it. "This is a travesty. A *travesty.*"

"It's a muffin, Zoey. A delicious muffin."

"Easy for you to say," Opal sniffed, pushing her own plate away. "It's a muffin, and it may be delicious, but it's a *liar*."

"It's easy to mix up blueberries and huckleberries when you're this late in the season," Sadie protested. *And you've eaten half of it.* "I've apologized and credited your accounts, but honestly ladies, when you called me out here, I didn't expect this was what I would get raked over the coals for."

"This is only round one," Ms. B informed her, a twinkle in her eye. "They're mad about the shootout, too." Born in Germany, Ms. B still had a soft German accent. It was the only soft thing about her. She was an older wiry white woman with a stern face and short blonde hair.

"I had nothing to do with that," Sadie said, sinking into her chair. "I was just unlucky."

Denise picked up her knitting somewhat regretfully, eyeing a few dropped stitches. "You seem to be unlucky often these days. What is this, number four?"

"Who's counting?" Gretchen said, smoothing the crease in her paperback page while the crease between her eyebrows deepened.

"Everyone," Zoey said. She pulled the plate closer to her and pulled off a piece of the wrongfully labeled actually blueberry not huckleberry muffin, popping it into her mouth. "It is good," she said, mouth full, nodding at Sadie.

"Even if you lied," Millie inputted, eyes still closed, and Sadie glared at her.

"So, are you going to find out who killed Malcolm then?" Opal interrupted. She'd given up pretense and was demolishing her comped muffin.

"I'm going to poke around," Sadie admitted. When she'd arrived at the bakery at seven for opening, she'd found out everyone in town already knew what had happened. She wasn't breaking the news to anyone. "I can't let them point the finger at my dad."

"Definitely not," Gretchen agreed.

"So, do y'all have any information for me?"

There was silence as they passed cagey looks around the table.

"Malcolm had a lot of enemies," Opal said finally. "When he forced his way into the Playhouse, he forced a few people out. And he threw a lot of money around. Maybe someone was after it." She wrapped the remains of her muffin up in a napkin, probably to give to Prada later.

"Plus the whole thing with Teton Tots." Chloe added.

"Did he have any friends?"

Silence.

"Oh! I've seen him and Ted Schultz out at lunch," Denise said.

"Ted Schultz of Schultz's Shirts? Pretty sure they're not friends. He had nothing nice to say about him while Malcolm was still getting CPR yesterday."

Denise shrugged. "They seemed friendly enough at lunch."

Interesting. Had they had a falling out?

"Well, that's a few leads, at least. You'll let me know if you hear anything?"

"Of course," her table of regulars chorused, and Sadie smiled at them. For all their ridiculous complaints, for all their picking at her and her business, these ladies truly loved her.

"Moose!" Max stuck their head through the pass through. "Need your help back here!"

Sadie stood. Back to work.

* * *

When Sadie returned to the kitchen, she realized what Max needed help with. It wasn't the baguettes they were shaping to prove. It wasn't helping Sage decorate the custom order of sugar cookies she was working on. It wasn't even tackling the pile of dishes. It was the woman devouring a ham and cheese croissant in her office while scrolling through her phone that had caused Max to call out.

"Penny, you're getting crumbs everywhere," Sadie admonished as she squeezed into the office. "Use a plate like a civilized person."

Penny, a white woman Sadie's age, brushed crumbs off her ample bosom, today clad in a ruffle-front button up with pink piping and paired with black high-waisted shorts with suspenders. Her hair was a riot of Barbie-pink curls around her head that matched her high-heeled pink wedges. "I'm starving," she complained around her last bite. "Randall's been riding me about details on this shootout thing."

"Why isn't Randall on the story?" Randall was the editor and chief reporter and photographer of the *Jackson Hole Journal*. It was a real one-man show except for Penny, his office manager, who had a wide ranging set of duties.

Penny pulled a pink compact out of her daisy-shaped purse and checked her lipstick. Still impeccable, of course. She blew a kiss into the mirror before snapping it closed and focusing her attention back on Sadie. "He tripped over his girlfriend's daughter's pet pig Fiona and broke his ankle, so the big baby's bossing me about from his desk."

"Missing another murder. Terrible luck he has."

"Unlike you, who never misses a murder, hmm?" Penny pulled out her reporter's notebook and activated the pink ink on her multi-color pen. With it poised over the pad, she adopted a professional expression. "Can I get a quote from you on what it was like when you opened the stagecoach door and Malcolm tumbled out on top of you, pinning you under his dying body?"

Sadie burst out a laugh. "That isn't what happened!"

"I've got three breathless tourists that swore up and down that's what they saw."

"And I'm sure you have video evidence that contradicts it."

Penny shrugged. "I'll leave those details to Randall. But really, girl, that must have been awful. How are you doing?"

"Blargh," Sadie groaned, leaning against the door behind her. Her office was a former closet, with just enough room for her desk, a chair, and a filing cabinet, and no extra chairs for visitors. Of which she wasn't, now that she thought of it. "Get out of my chair," she groused. "I've been standing for hours."

Penny rolled her eyes behind her glitter-pink cat-eye glasses, but obliged, more crumbs falling from her lap as she stood and squeezed by Sadie.

"Tell you what." Penny tucked her notebook back into her purse. "You tell me what you know, and I'll tell you what I know."

"You go first."

"You drive a hard bargain, Moose."

"Always have."

"Fine. Toxicology report on Malcolm says he had high levels of ivermectin in his system. Apparently, that's some sort of para-site-fighting medicine."

"What?"

"I know," Penny said, frowning. "He died of heart failure, but according to his doctor, they did not prescribe him anything for parasites, so that's one reason they're considering poisoning."

"Huh."

"Did you notice anything strange about Malcolm before the act yesterday?"

Sadie considered it. "He was cheerful enough, if a little

nervous. He was...sweaty, but we all were? And he was popping antacids like they were candy, said he had an upset stomach. And he coughed some. He did seem unwell, to be honest. There was one part during the act that he seemed a little unsteady on his feet, too."

"I talked to your dad—"

"Penny!"

"Well, of course I did. Anyway, he said Malcolm flubbed his lines a couple times, which was unlike him. Though he was an awful actor, he at least remembered his lines."

"I didn't notice, but I only read the part of the script I needed to memorize."

"Right, right, 'help, please!'" Penny cried dramatically.

There was a knock on the door, then Max's voice. "All good in there?"

"Penny's just making fun of me. We're good," Sadie assured them through the door.

"Besides my dad, who else does the PD suspect?"

"Why do you presume I know anything about what the PD thinks?"

"Maybe because you've moved in with Officer Greg Knott himself? Don't tell me he doesn't pillow talk with you."

Penny had the decency to blush. "Well, off the record, of course..."

"I'm the one that's supposed to say that part. Which reminds me, don't quote me on anything please? I don't need more attention than I'm already getting."

"Fine, fine," Penny agreed. "Anyway, besides your dad, they're looking closely at everyone else at the show save for you since you were a last-minute addition and Will Nolan has a crush on you—"

"Penny!"

"It doesn't matter how many times you say that, I'm still

going to keep talking. Anyway, you seem off the hook. They're also questioning the Playhouse director Helen Foster and her husband, former leading man Bob, the daycare director, and friends and family of Malcolm."

"Did he have friends and family?"

Penny shook her head. "His family is in California and he spends his daddy's money here. Friends are sparse, no roommates or girlfriends. His entire life seems like it was making it big in the Jackson Hole acting scene, which is...not much of a life goal when I consider it."

"Everyone wants different things in life, Penny," Sadie said. "But that's not much to go on."

"Nope, especially because you apparently have nothing for me."

"Wrong place wrong time for me."

"But you're looking into it anyway...?"

"Just call me Sadie Moose, Saloon Girl Detective."

Chapter Six

K nowing the investigation would eat up the next few days, Sadie took the afternoon at the bakery to get caught up on admin work. There was always more than enough of it to go around. Between the bakery, the thriving custom order business, and the three coffee kiosks she'd started with her business partners, Kendall and her fiancé Claire Cabot, in the last year, there was always something her accountant or lawyers needed from her to keep the business moving. Sadie examined the queue of custom orders that had come in off the website and worried over the scheduling. With the baked goods for the coffee kiosks and the bakery coming from one kitchen, things were getting tight.

She dialed Claire on her cell phone.

After a ring, Claire's smooth, sophisticated hello came through the line.

"Hey Claire," Sadie said. "What's up?"

"I'm in between meetings. What's going on with you?"

"Wanted to check in on the construction plans for the Wilson building." Last winter, when Sadie had entered the partnership with Kendall and Claire to run the coffee kiosks,

Claire had purchased a former office building in Wilson, a town fifteen minutes to the west of Jackson at the base of Teton Pass. Commuters from the Idaho towns of Victor, Driggs, and others, priced out of Jackson housing—which, who wasn't, honestly— were their main kiosk customers, and the building had the perfect location for easy on and off from the highway. After a lot of planning, they'd decided to convert the building into a commercial bakery to take the pressure off the Jackson location. As a bonus, they would convert the second floor into apartments for employee housing. But construction was taking longer than any of them had hoped.

"The crew is supposed to start demo next week. Kendall's begging to swing a sledgehammer, so I'm sure you'll hear all about it once they start," Claire said. "Did you check the current timeline on the remote workspace?"

Sadie groaned. Right. The remote workspace. Claire's efficiency—and that of her virtual assistant, Lane—put Sadie to shame. "I should've checked there before I bugged you. Sorry Claire."

"That's okay," Claire said gently. "I'll have Lane send you the login information again, just in case."

That was probably sorely needed. Sadie couldn't remember the last time she'd logged in. "Thanks, Claire. I'll let you go."

Claire cleared her throat. "Um, before you go, I did have a question for you."

Sadie's interest was piqued. Claire never sounded uncertain, so the vulnerable note in her voice was a surprise. "Of course, go ahead."

"Has Kendall...said anything to you about the wedding?"

"What hasn't she said to me about the wedding?" Sadie laughed. "The last plans I heard were a spontaneous float trip with you two saying vows during the hardest class of rapids."

Claire laughed weakly. "I shot that idea down a while ago.

So...she's still talking about it?"

Sadie was puzzled. "Yeah. She's so excited. Why would you wonder?"

"Oh...I don't know. I feel like she hasn't been wanting to talk about plans lately. I just really want to marry her, you know? Are all the different ideas her way of...putting it off?"

Sadie considered that. Kendall had the laser-sharp focus of a surgeon in the operating room and the attention span of a squirrel, so if you weren't paying attention, she could lose you with where she was going sometimes. "I think if you're concerned, you need to talk to Kendall about it, not me," Sadie said not unkindly. She really didn't want to be in the middle. "But I know Kendall seems just as excited about marrying you today as she was that day you both asked each other simultaneously in the park on Valentine's Day. Could be she's just...overwhelmed with options. She loves possibilities, you know? Maybe y'all can narrow down the range for her so she can focus more."

"You're right," Claire said, sounding relieved. "That's a good idea. I'll talk to her about it."

After chatting a few more minutes, they hung up, and Sadie spent the next few hours in spreadsheet purgatory. When she pulled herself out of it, it was closing time. She logged off her computer and went to help Max prep for the next day and clean up. She'd gotten caught up enough at her day job. Tonight, her investigation would begin.

* * *

After the uproar of the last twenty-four hours, Sadie felt lousy she hadn't checked in with Paige on the childcare situation, so she texted her to meet up at the farmer's market that evening. Held in the parking lot of Snow King, the ski hill at the south side of town, it was a local's favorite summer activity. Sadie biked over, leaving Tyrone at home even though he looked at her with big brown moosey eyes. The market was strictly no dogs allowed.

After parking and locking her bike, Sadie wandered around, looking for her friend. She waved at Denise Garza, who was doing a brisk business in her knitted baby and toddler visors. She stopped to chat with her friend Nash, who was pulling drafts at the brewpub's traveling beer trailer and charming customers. Kamari was staffing a booth raising money for the kid's ski team. She was one of their coaches, and judging by the crowd of kids around her asking when the ski movie she'd wrapped last winter was debuting, also one of their favorites. She stopped at the ShelterJH booth and dropped some change into their donation jar. The organization built support and political power to address housing insecurity in the area, and she supported them whenever she could. Too many people couldn't afford to live where they worked, and she was sick of billionaires moving in and slamming the door shut behind them.

Past the food trucks, non-profits, and vendors were the farmer's booths. The abundance of produce made Sadie's mind race with possibilities, and she picked up a few bunches of colorful rainbow chard and scallions for the bakery's next quiche of the day. While she perused an array of heirloom tomatoes, she overheard Gavin at the next booth having an intense discussion with a mushroom farmer.

"Smell this," he demanded when he saw her, shoving a handful of alien-looking mushrooms into her face.

Sadie wrinkled her nose. "Um...yum?"

"Imbecile," Gavin grumbled, turning back to the farmer with a glint in his eye. Sadie knew that glint and backed away. She didn't want to be associated with Gavin's cutthroat haggling.

Kendall was at the public library's bicycle-powered book

cart, thumbing through a kid's book on bats.

"Hit me with a bat fact, friend," Sadie requested as she stopped next to her, scanning the titles on offer.

"Did you know bats can live up to thirty years?"

"I did not," Sadie mused. "How interesting. Have you seen Paige around?"

"Over by the playground, I think," Kendall said, sliding the book back on the shelf. She was distracted.

"You okay?"

"Yeah, I'm good. Claire said she wanted to talk tonight when she was done with her meetings, like she doesn't know that I'll spend the rest of the day worried about what she wants to talk about."

Sadie patted her arm. "She loves you. I'm sure it's no big deal." At least, Sadie hoped it wouldn't be. It wasn't often Claire and Kendall weren't in sync.

Kendall brightened. "You're right, she does love me. I mean, who doesn't? Hey, what do you think about officiating our wedding?"

Sadie blinked. "Uh...I've never done that before?"

"You'd be great at it. But do you scuba?"

Sadie spent the next few minutes explaining to Kendall that no, she did not scuba, and no, she would not learn because she got claustrophobic easily, and yes, she would consider officiating the wedding if they both wanted her to, but no, she would not do it while skydiving, cliff diving, or parasailing, so maybe consider something less death-defying to convince her.

"You're no fun," Kendall groused good-naturedly. "I'm going to get a beer." She wandered off, so Sadie headed for the playground.

Right away, she spotted Paige and Mateo. Luna was strapped to Mateo's chest while he ate an ice cream cone over her head. Paige was talking to another woman with several children running around playing at the nearby playground. Paige was wearing a Gates-Ortiz for Mayor shirt and had a folder Sadie knew was full of voter registration forms under her arm. She was so proud of her friend. Paige had been on the town council for four years, and with the announcement of the long-time-Mayor's retirement this summer, she was fighting a tough campaign against her opponent, billionaire land developer Wade Fisher. Based on the primary numbers, Sadie thought Paige had it in the bag, but there were still two and a half months until Election Day. A lot could happen between now and then.

"Hey, you bring one of those shirts for me?" Sadie asked as she walked up next to Paige. Paige reached into her backpack and handed her one, distractedly, still talking earnestly to the other woman.

"—unfortunately there doesn't appear to be anything the council can do. Now it's up to Malcolm's heir, whoever that may be," Paige was saying.

"I heard none of it was his money, anyway. I bet his dad is really in control. And he doesn't even live here! Maybe we should send him a letter," the woman said fretfully.

Sadie pulled the shirt over her tank top and shook out her hair. There. Now she was riding for the brand. "Appealing to him isn't a bad idea," she said when there was a break in conversation. "Could you get the center to film a video featuring the kids with information on how many people this will hurt, and how difficult and expensive it will be to find a new building, and then send it to him?"

"Post it on YouTube and tag him," Mateo said, bouncing up and down in an attempt to shush Luna, who was starting to squawk.

"YouTube, Twitter, Facebook, TikTok..." Paige ticked the options off her fingers. "That's not a bad idea, Sadie. Maybe we can publicly shame Malcolm's dad into stepping in and canceling the eviction."

"Sadie Moose?" The woman's gaze sharpened on Sadie. She was a white woman, tall and thin, with a blonde ponytail shoved under a runner's cap. She looked like she'd run to the park from her athletic gear, and Sadie guessed the triple-wide jogging stroller parked nearby was hers.

"That's me," Sadie said, holding out her hand. The woman shook it.

"I'm Vivian Benson, the director of Teton Tots."

"Oh, nice to meet you," Sadie said. "I'm sorry about all this. Malcolm made a mess of things, didn't he?"

Vivian scoffed. "That man was a real son of a—" she glanced around at the kids nearby "—donkey, I tell you what. We dealt with his complaints about the center for years. We installed a higher fence between his property and ours. We planted new trees to help dampen the sound of our kids outside. We stopped blowing bubbles if the wind was going in his direction. We drew the line at his requests that we stop singing, stop talking, and stop playing." She rolled her eyes. "And now he's dead, and he's still causing us trouble!"

"Wow," Sadie said. "I didn't know you had so much history with him. When was the last time you talked to him?"

A toddler in a Spiderman costume ran up to Vivian asking for a snack, distracting her, and Paige caught her attention.

"Are you really going to question her here?" She hissed.

Sadie shrugged. "I'll be gentle. I just want to know more about Malcolm."

"Please be subtle. She's a nice woman and this has her totally stressed out."

Vivian returned to the circle. "I saw Malcolm yesterday morning. We'd just been served with the lease termination notice, and I was frantic. I went to his condo to confront him, but he wouldn't speak to me. He opened the door a crack and told me all communication needed to go through his lawyer. Sounded like hell, too."

"Really? In what way?"

"He was coughing a lot. I was worried he had Covid, actually." Vivian shuddered. "And for all he was coughing, he was still sucking on that stupid vape pen."

"Huh. Did you contact his lawyer?"

"Our lawyer is handling it. But I think taking it directly into our own hands, appealing publicly, is a good idea."

"Let me know if I can help," Sadie said. "The bakery has a broad social media following. We can amplify the message."

"Thanks for that," Vivian said. Her watch beeped at her, and she glanced at it before turning to the playground to call out to her kids that it was time to go. With amazing efficiency, she loaded them into the triple stroller, tallest to shortest with Spiderman in the middle, then got them each settled with a snack and water bottle and jogged away, waving.

"She's amazing," Paige said from beside her. "My mom mentor."

"You're an amazing mom," Sadie said, giving Paige a hug. "How are you doing with all this?"

Paige sighed heavily. "Not good, honestly. I feel so overwhelmed. Luna's only two months old but I'm starting to think about going back to my practice part-time and this campaign is hanging over my head. And now childcare is an unknown."

"It's a lot," Sadie agreed. "I'm here for you while you figure it all out."

Paige gave her a half smile. "That's what I love about you, Sadie Moose. You know I can do it, and you're my biggest cheerleader and hand holder. Thanks for being you. Now, wipe your eyes and let's go get some pad Thai. I feel like getting my ass kicked by Malee's five-star spice."

Chapter Seven

L ater that night, mouth still burning from the pad thai she'd eaten from the Get Rich or Thai Tryin' food truck, Sadie decided she'd do some research out on her back deck. The sun had dropped below the mountains, and it was cool out. And because she'd witnessed a death and found out her father was a suspect in said death in the last twenty-four hours, she brought a bottle of red wine out on the deck along with her laptop and notebook.

Tyrone danced around her feet as she sat, so she got back up to find the ball thrower so she could throw balls for him while she relaxed. She poured a glass of wine and threw a ball for Tyrone, taking a healthy gulp.

Arlo had attended a formal interview with the police department that afternoon, according to a text she'd gotten from him. Mateo had sent a colleague with him. Arlo said it had been uneventful, and Sadie hoped that was true, and suspicion was off him for good. But just in case, she'd stay on the case. First on her list of things to research was to look up the article Penny had written for the *Journal*. She navigated to the webpage, cursed the pop-up ads, then finally pulled it up.

SHOOTOUT DEATH CAUSED BY POISONING read the headline. Sadie scanned it. Nothing she didn't already know. Bummer.

Next, she opened Facebook. Time to do a deep dive on Malcolm and who his friends may have been.

A glass of wine later, Sadie had scoured Malcolm's socials and felt stymied. What she knew about Malcolm after an hour's worth of research on his digital presence was unhelpful. He was thirty-eight, single, never married. He was the son of a Silicon Valley tech billionaire, but he'd grown up in Gilroy, California, a relatively small town she only knew of because of its annual Garlic Festival. He'd lived in LA for a few years, but he didn't have a profile on IMDB and she didn't find any news of him acting in the theater there. Really, there wasn't much about him until he'd moved to Jackson permanently four years ago. His East Jackson condo showed it was owned by TTSH LLC, probably a company his dad owned, and Zillow estimated it was worth close to $1.5 million.

According to his Instagram, he frequented the gym Kendall went to, so she'd put Kendall on that. He dined at the fancier restaurants in town, so she'd put Gavin on those. He spent most of his time at the Playhouse, it seemed. He was on the board of directors for it, and she found several articles about donations he'd made to the theater, including financing the restoration of the stagecoach for the shootout.

Sadie scanned the webpage that listed the board of directors. She was surprised to see Ted Schultz's name. He wasn't much of a patron of the arts, from what she knew of him. But once she thought about it, she could see him being involved because of the tourist-driven nature of his business. Schultz's Shirts had occupied the building at the corner of Cache and Broadway on the town square since the nineties. The shootout happened right in front of his shop, and he counted on tourists who watched the show to come in and buy Jackson Hole merchandise. Sadie definitely needed to talk to him.

Sipping the last of her glass of wine, she finished her list of people to talk to:

• Gym scene: Kendall

• Restaurant scene: Gavin

• Juliana

• Helen Foster, Playhouse Director

• Ted Schultz

• Cody (stagecoach driver)

• Robber #1, #2, #3 - names?!

• Vivian Benson

It was a long list, and she wasn't sure where she'd find the time to talk to everyone on it. But the only way to get started was to get started. Tyrone had settled at her feet and she slipped a foot out of its sandal to give him a tummy rub with her foot. He made a happy sound, and she smiled at him. It was a cool night, a welcome respite from the hot temperatures of the afternoon. The sun had disappeared behind the butte, and the twinkle lights she'd strung in her backyard were twinkling. It was a perfect Jackson Hole summer night. She poured another glass of wine and shut her laptop. Tomorrow she'd tackle her list. For now, she could relax.

Her phone buzzed, and she glanced at it.

It was from an unknown number, a simple message.

STAY OUT OF IT.

Sadie stared at the message. Quickly, she typed the phone number it had come from into her phone's search engine. Zero results.

She tried calling it. Out of service.

Whoever had texted her had used a spoofed number.

Tyrone leapt to his feet to bark at the back gate and Sadie put her phone down with a clatter, heart racing. Someone was out in the alley.

* * *

"You did say we could fight more today," Sadie said, relief filling her when Will, not a threatening stranger, walked through the gate. He was in street clothes, no police department hat or vest.

He flashed a grin at her as he mounted the steps to the deck and took a seat across from her at the patio table. "I had an interesting day and thought you might want to hear about it."

Sadie raised her eyebrows. He was offering her information? "Can I offer you a glass of wine? Cold pizza?"

"As long as you don't count it as a date."

Sadie rolled her eyes at him, unwilling to get into *that* again. She stood. "Throw the ball for Tyrone. I'll be back in a few."

When she returned, plates of cold pizza and an extra wineglass in hand, Will was studying her list while Tyrone danced at his feet, nudging the ball with his nose. Absently, he threw the ball again, then pushed the list out of the way so she could put the plate in front of him.

"Why Ted Schultz?" He asked when she'd sat down.

Sadie took a bite of a buffalo chicken slice and pulled the list towards her. She wasn't sure how she felt about him snooping like that. Was he doing it as a cop investigating the case, or as a friend? That was what made her nervous about Will, she realized. She didn't know when or if he turned his cop off. Was he always judging? Always building a case? Sadie knew Will was a good guy. When he'd first moved to Jackson and found out the police department was boycotting her bakery because of the Black Lives Matter sticker on the door, he'd done something about it. Plenty of officers frequented the bakery now, and they contracted with her to provide treats for staff meetings once a month. She knew Will had supported policies the new police chief had put into place to reduce discriminatory practices. He was a good cop. But he was still a cop.

Were her friends safe around him? That's what worried her the most. Kendall always had knowledge she couldn't possibly get through above-board means. Kamari was a Black woman in a mostly white town. Max was non-binary and Native American. Sage definitely used marijuana, and that was still very illegal in Wyoming.

"I can tell you're worrying about something," Will said across from her, a slice of jalapeño and pineapple pizza in his hand.

Did she confess her fears? "Are you off duty right now?" She asked.

He put down his pizza and uncorked the wine, pouring himself a glass, then taking a pointed sip. "Yep."

"So when you come here and you're off duty and then you look at my list, are you looking as a friend or as a cop?"

"I'm always a cop. I'm always investigating. But I'm here as a friend."

"That confuses me."

"If you weren't always somehow at the center of my investigations, it wouldn't be so confusing."

Sadie prickled at that. Like she chose these things. Like she liked always being in the wrong place at the wrong time.

"I was joking, Sadie," Will said before she could snap at him. He put his hand out, covering hers. It was warm in the cool night. Unbidden, her hand turned in his, and they were palm to palm. They were...holding hands. Huh.

"Ted Schultz is on the board of directors at the Playhouse, and someone told me he thought he was a friend of Malcolm's, but right after I found Malcolm, Ted was saying some not-nice things about him, so I think it's worth talking to him."

Will's gaze sharpened. "He was saying unkind things? He didn't tell us that."

Sadie pulled her hand away from his. Right. Investigating. Always. "Yeah, he called him a 'no-talent over-actor' and didn't seem upset about it at all." She picked up her list where he'd pushed it away and looked over it again. "Anyone else on here surprise you?"

He shook his head. "Nope."

"Any of them suspects?"

"Can't answer that yet."

"Anything new to tell me? You told me you had an interesting day."

Will took a sip of his wine.

"Well, I'm sure you've heard the toxin in his body was an anti-parasite medication?"

Sadie nodded.

"It's unclear how he got a hold of it. No doctor had prescribed it. There were no pills in his house or car. We're testing some personal items to see if he might have come into contact with it that way."

"Is that kind of drug something that you would need to consume over time and it gradually builds up to a level than can kill you, or something he would have had to take immediately before?"

"We think it built up in him over a period of time."

"Did you test his TUMS?"

Will grinned at her. "Clever girl. We're doing that. He was found with those on him."

"Does he have family coming into town for some sort of service?"

"We haven't released the body yet, but they have instructed us to send it to the mortuary. I don't know about anything else."

"Huh. He didn't seem close to anyone looking through his social media. It's kind of sad. His life was the Playhouse, but many people there didn't like him."

"From what I heard, he earned the dislike."

That seemed cold to Sadie, but she'd been known to care too much in the past. Sadie opened her mouth to ask another question, but Will held up a hand. "That's about all I can say for now. And for the love, please don't repeat those things to Penny, will ya? I have a hard enough time with Greg."

"I promise nothing." Sadie shrugged.

Will's face sobered. "But do be careful, okay, Sadie? I know I won't stop you from investigating. I don't want to stop you. You have a way of finding things out, and I appreciate when you share with me. But just...be careful, okay?"

Sadie thought of the text message. She'd caught someone's attention already, and she hadn't really started asking questions. But of course she would be careful. She was always careful. This time wouldn't be any different.

Chapter Eight

On Thursday mornings, Juliana worked at Bad Hair Day, an exclusive salon in downtown Jackson. It was only a few blocks away from the bakery, so after Sadie helped through the morning rush and distributed the custom orders for the weekend to Max and Sage, she set off in that direction. It was warm, with a high forecasted in the nineties, but the morning had the crisp feel that meant autumn was right around the corner. The sun was at a different angle, too, and everything was bathed in a golden light. The distant haze of smoke from a nearby wildfire added to the effect.

Thinking of fires made her think of Jake Moreno, her ex-boyfriend who was a wildland firefighter. They'd broken up this winter when Jake found out he had a surprise preteen daughter. The last she'd spoken to him, his daughter, Astrid, and her mom, Victoria, were living with him while they figured things out. Breaking up with him had been confusing and sad, but in the end, amicable, and they were still friends. She wondered how he was fairing during fire season. She pulled out her phone and sent him a quick text.

Smoke in the air makes me think of you. How are
you doing? Astrid starts school soon?

She didn't expect to hear from him instantly, so she put her phone back in her pocket. When he was out on fires, he could take weeks to reply. But at least she'd tried.

Will had texted her this morning, a meme of Jessica Fletcher from Murder She Wrote holding a phone to her ear and grinning with the caption, WHO'S DEAD? It had made her laugh, and she felt some of the tension she'd been holding on to about the nature of their tenuous friendship and whatever else might be going on loosen.

She was a block away from the salon when she heard her name shouted behind her.

"Sadie! Sadie!"

She turned to look and gaped when Paige came rushing up to her, red in the face. Her calm, always-cool-and-collected wellness coach and therapist bestie certainly had been frantic lately. Sadie attributed it to the adorable nugget strapped to her chest. *She may be little, but she was fierce.*

"What's wrong, Paige?" Sadie asked, concerned.

But Paige wasn't listening. She was unbuckling her carrier and handing it to her. "Put this on," she said, clutching Luna to her chest. Luna sucked her fist without concern, her eyes shaded by the teal baby visor Denise had knitted her.

"Uhh..." Sadie eyed the contraption, finding the belt adjuster and letting it out so it fit around her much bigger waist, then clipping it behind her. "What's going on?"

Paige plopped Luna into her arms and bustled around her, pulling the arm straps up and over her arms and buckling the top strap, then sticking her hands into the carrier to adjust Luna's positioning.

"Ouch," Sadie complained as Paige poked her tummy.

"Sorry, sorry," Paige muttered. She leaned in and kissed Luna's head. "She needs to be close enough to kiss, okay? That's how you know she's safe in there. Kiss her. Can you kiss her?"

Sadie leaned her head forward to brush a kiss on Luna's soft head, her straight, fine black hair tickling her lips.

"Good, good," Paige said, standing back. "Oh, and you'll need this." She took off her oversize fanny pack and slung it around Sadie's hips, adjusting it. "There are diapers in there and a couple bottles of formula you just add water to." She took hold of Sadie's face and pulled it close to hers, staring into her eyes fiercely. "Make sure the water is slightly warmer than room temperature but not too hot, do you understand?"

Sadie gazed into her best friend's intense gaze and nodded slowly. "I understand. Slightly warmer than room temperature, but not too hot. I got it. Diapers inside. Formula bottles. Change of clothes in case of blow out?"

"Of course," Paige said, satisfied. She took a breath and blew out, her strawberry blonde bangs fluttering. "Now, I'm off to a candidate forum. Wade apparently 'forgot' to tell me about it, and is busy telling everyone there how I didn't bother to show up. Caught him on Facebook Live though, so I'm going to crash it."

Sadie bristled at that. "What an asshole. Get him, girl. I've got Luna."

"Thanks, Sadie," Paige called, already bustling down the street away from her.

Sadie looked down at the baby strapped securely to her, pulling up the visor so she could see her eyes. She was happily curled in, eyes closed, sucking her fist. Well. "I've never had a baby as a sidekick before," she whispered to her. "Something tells me you'll be good at getting people to talk."

In answer, Luna filled her diaper loudly.

"Perfect," Sadie said, crinkling her nose. "Let's go, Stinky."

* * *

Thankfully, the salon had a changing table in the restroom, so fifteen sweaty minutes later, Sadie emerged from the bathroom with a cleaned up Luna, though getting her back into the carrier seemed like a lost cause.

Juliana clucked her tongue at her from where she was sweeping hair into a pile to vacuum it up. "Where'd you get that baby, girl?"

"This is Luna, my friend Paige's daughter."

"Oh, Paige Running for Mayor Paige?"

"That's her."

"Tell her she has my vote. That Wade Fisher is bad news for this town."

"Agreed, and I will."

Juliana waved at the chair. "Sit down and tell me what you're here for."

Sadie balked. "Oh, I just wanted to talk..."

"Mmmhmm," Juliana said, pulling her into the chair. "My next appointment cancelled and I'll dish all you want about Malcolm, but you gotta make it worth my time."

Sadie sighed and sat, adjusting Luna, who'd fallen back asleep, in her lap. "I guess I could use a trim."

Juliana eyed the ends of Sadie's long, straight, brown hair and made a face. "Six inches minimum. And some shaping."

"Fine, fine. But you better spill."

Minutes later, draped with a cape, Luna settled on top of Sadie's propped up legs, Juliana started snipping...and sniping.

According to her, Malcolm had used his daddy's money to leverage his way into the theater company, buying a board of directors seat for the cost of a new sound and lighting system and the lead in the shootout for the cost of a restored stagecoach.

"Who did he step over on the way?" Sadie glanced at a lock

of hair on the floor and frowned, twisting around to glimpse herself in the mirror. "Six inches, right?"

"Of course," Juliana said, forcibly tipping her head back around. "Well, who didn't he step over is a better question, but his most vocal critic was Helen Foster."

"The director of the Playhouse? You would think she'd be more friendly considering he paid for so much stuff."

"Yes, and since he was on the board, he technically had a say over her performance, but Helen never got over him replacing her husband as the Playhouse's go-to leading man."

"Ahh." Sadie had thought the same thing when she found out Malcolm was the new lead.

"Yep. One time, I heard Bob and Malcolm arguing and whoooooeeeee it was something. I thought they were going to punch each other!"

"When was that?"

"Oh, more than once, but most recently, a few weeks ago. During the choreography of the new shootout. Bob was teaching Malcolm his old moves, but Malcolm wanted to do some edgier stuff."

"Oh, like the falling off the stagecoach stuff? That was pretty technical."

"Mmmhmm." *Snip, snip* went her scissors. Sadie's head was feeling abnormally light. She was getting a bad feeling about this. "Malcolm told Bob he didn't need his 'old man moves' and Bob told him he needed some 'old man respect' and it really devolved from there. Arlo actually broke it up."

"I'll need to ask Dad about that, then." Sadie frowned. Arlo hadn't said much to her about Malcolm at all, now that she thought about it. She needed to corner him and get answers out of him. "Did Malcolm have any more enemies?"

"Well, he used to be best friends with Ted Schultz, but the

two of them had a falling out over politics during the pandemic and it got nuclear."

"Ted's a real red hat guy," Sadie grimaced. "Remember the stink he raised about masks during the height of everything?"

Juliana snorted. She'd switched to a different type of scissor and was making artful, tiny snips. "That man is the most gullible in the world. He hasn't met a conspiracy theory he didn't immediately believe in. I heard him and his wife talking seriously about lizard people at the taqueria the other day. And have you looked, really looked, at what they sell in his shop these days? It gives our town a bad name."

Sadie hadn't noticed when she'd taken shelter there on Tuesday. Sounded like she needed to go by and check out the merchandise as well as talk to Ted.

"There," Juliana said, putting the scissors down. She put some balm in her hands and rubbed them together, then started fluffing Sadie's too-light hair.

"Can I see now?"

"Almost," Juliana said, scrunching with concentration. Luna was starting to squirm on Sadie's lap. Finally, Juliana twirled her around in the chair. "Ta da!"

Sadie blinked at herself, then reached forward to grab her glasses off the counter and slip them on. Juliana had cut more like ten inches than six and had added texture where there was usually none. "How did you get it all wavy like that?"

"I took the weight off the ends, textured it, and scrunched a little. It was so heavy before it had no choice but to be straight."

"It looks...fantastic." Sadie picked up Luna, shushing her.

"You're a new woman, Sadie Moose," Juliana said, smiling. She whipped off the cloak. "That'll be $128.50."

Chapter Nine

Once Sadie recovered from the shock of a Jackson Hole-priced haircut, she let Juliana add new products to the total, too. Juliana helped her back into the baby carrier, then shooed her away as her next client came through the door.

Out on the sidewalk, Sadie marveled at how lightweight her head felt. She was swishing her head back and forth, enjoying the feeling and trying to decide where to head next when she spotted an older white woman in a bright red Jackson Hole Playhouse t-shirt walking across the street. Sadie looked both ways and rushed across the street to intercept her.

"Helen!"

The woman stopped, an annoyed look on her face. "Sadie. I'm sorry, I don't have a lot of time to chat. I'm headed to an emergency board meeting and I'm getting stopped every six feet by gossips."

Sadie gulped. "Oh, I don't want gossip," she hedged. She titled to the side so Helen could see Luna's sweet face, hoping that might win her over. The woman's face softened a margin.

"Is that Paige and Mateo's new baby?"

"It is, baby Luna. Isn't she the sweetest?"

Helen cooed over her and her adorable visor.

"I wanted to tell you how sorry I am about Malcolm."

Helen sighed heavily. "Thank you. And I'm sorry for how your debut in the shootout went. Thank you for standing in, by the way."

"It wasn't how I pictured it going for sure," Sadie admitted. "How long had you known Malcolm?"

Helen pursed her lips. "He moved here four or five years ago and immediately started hanging around. He had a background in the Northern California theater scene with some minor credits and started trying out for roles."

"Were you friends?"

"We were professional colleagues," Helen said, straightening. "His loss will reverberate throughout the theater scene in this town and is a tremendous blow to the Playhouse."

"He donated a lot of money over the years," Sadie said, watching Helen closely.

Helen's face flushed. "His contributions were multi-faceted. Now, I must be on my way."

"Have a nice day," Sadie said, watching her leave. She had wanted to ask how Bob felt about Malcolm's death, but she hadn't gotten the opportunity. Maybe she could track him down later in the day.

She and Luna set off towards Sadie's house. She had a feeling Arlo would be home, and it was time to ask him a few more questions.

She found him in the backyard of the house they were renting from her. Arlo was in his hammock, headphones on, reading a *SKI* magazine. Really, Sadie should've made sure he saw her before she poked his backside. He was an old man. He could've broken a hip. But watching him flip out of the hammock screeching but landing on his feet was worth it. Sadie laughed so hard Luna started crying.

"Awww," Arlo cooed, immediately forgetting Sadie's transgression with a baby nearby. "Come to your honorary Papa, sweet Luna," he said, deftly unclipping the baby carrier from Sadie and cuddling Luna to his chest. "She's hungry," he observed.

"How do you know that?" Sadie asked.

"She's cramming two fists in her mouth while she wails," Arlo said dryly. "I presume Paige sent you with a bottle?"

Sadie patted her fanny pack. "I'm fully outfitted."

"Then in we go. It's too hot out here for a baby, even one with an adorable visor." Arlo ushered her inside. "Nice haircut, by the way."

"Thanks, Dad."

Inside, Sadie prepared the bottle under Arlo's strict supervision, proving not once but twice that the water was warmer than room temperature but not too hot, before handing it to him along with a burp cloth from the seemingly bottomless fanny pack. They settled into the living room, Luna sucking at the bottle while Arlo exclaimed like she was solving quadratic equations. Sadie narrowed her eyes at him. He and her mom had never once pressured her about having grandkids. They'd never commented on her dating life except to make a joke, usually at their own expense, since she was in high school. But this behavior? This was not the behavior of a sixty-plus-year-old-man who *didn't* want grandkids.

"Don't worry, Sadie-doll," Arlo laughed. "This will fill my prospective-Papa tank for months. Maybe years. No rush. If you decide to have kids at all."

"You really are the best. You know that, right?"

Arlo puffed out his chest. "I always have been, even when you were a teenager, and you hated me."

"I never hated you."

"Could've fooled me," he said to Luna in a sing-songy voice. "Now, I take it you're here to ask me some questions. Go ahead. Make my day."

Once Dirty Arlo, always Dirty Arlo.

"I heard you broke up a fight between Malcolm and Bob Foster a few weeks ago."

"That I did. We were working on choreography, and Malcolm was insulting Bob's advice. Bob didn't take kindly to it, and they almost came to blows. Me and Cody broke them up."

"What happened after that?"

"Bob left. He hasn't been back to the Playhouse since, from what I understand. Malcolm changed the choreography to what you saw on Tuesday. It was difficult, and edgy, and the crowd loved it, so I think he was on to something."

"Do you think Bob was mad enough to murder Malcolm?"

"Bob Foster, the overly emotional actor with a bad leg and a heart condition? No. I don't think so."

"Malcolm was poisoned. Doesn't take a lot of physical strength to do that, just malice and some discretion."

"And some smarts. And Bob may be an excellent leading man that worked stages on both sides of the pond in his younger years, but he's not what I'd call a *smart* man. He still mixes up stage left and right sometimes."

"Hmm."

"Now, someone with the smarts to kill Malcolm *and* the malice? Besides me, of course?"

"Dad!"

"Kidding, kidding." He popped the bottle from Luna's mouth and put her on his shoulder to burp her. "Helen. Helen has malice and duplicity for days, and she hates that Malcolm forced Bob out."

"I just saw Helen on the street. She seemed distracted but

tight lipped. Also, she's in charge. How come she didn't prevent Malcolm getting the lead roles?"

"Money talks. The board of directors stepped in more than once on behalf of Malcolm and overrode Helen's casting decisions. Malcolm would threaten to leave, taking his dad's wallet with him, and the board would give in to whatever he wanted. Helen threatened to quit more than once, but what would she have done? They have that beautiful property in Wilson you know, they don't want to move, and acting is Bob's life and directing is Helen's dream. I think she hoped Malcolm would just...get bored and move on. Like a typical playboy."

"But he never did..."

"So maybe she decided to get rid of him once and for all."

"Makes sense," Sadie said.

"It would," Arlo agreed, thumping Luna's back a little harder. "Except Helen was out of town until this morning. She left over a week ago when her elderly sister fell and broke a hip, and she flew out to be with her."

"Oh."

"Yeah."

"The police think the poison was given over a period of time before it took Malcolm out, like a week, so maybe?"

"Maybe."

"*Braaaaaaaaaaaaaaaaaaaaap!*"

Sadie jumped, staring at Luna. She had no idea small babies could make such loud noises. Arlo was praising her like she'd discovered the formula for cold fusion. He settled her back in his lap to give her the second half of the bottle.

"Anyone else you can think of that had a grudge against Malcolm?"

Arlo considered. "Not that I can think of. He wasn't an amiable man, very self-involved, with no ability to self-reflect or take criticism. But despite all that, he seemed harmless to me. An overly rich brat who'd never grown up and took what he wanted by any means necessary just because he could."

Sadie heard a noise from the back door, then the sound of a bag being dumped on the floor. Her mom came into view through the kitchen, dressed in her golf gear.

"Ah, Sadie," she said. "Glad you're here. You won't believe what I just heard on green six."

* * *

Over a hastily put together lunch of sandwiches, chips, and fruit, Robin shared her story. Luna was on her back on the floor, a thick blanket cushioning her body while she kicked her arms and legs and stared down the ceiling fan. Sadie watched her closely while she devoured her sandwich. Investigating was work that built up an appetite.

"Sherry's sick, so Tootsie brought in a friend to fill out our foursome," Robin was saying. "She's a flashy lady, all expensive and matchy-matchy. Rock on her finger that barely fit under a golf glove. Big hair. Red lipstick. Nice, though."

Sadie crunched a chip while she waited for her mom to get to the point.

"Turns out, she's the wife of the man that owns the stock at the Jackson Hole Rodeo."

Arlo whistled. "Fancy."

"What's that mean, exactly?" Sadie asked.

"A contractor puts the rodeo on. The current contractor subcontracts the rodeo stock. I've seen the budget. That's big money."

"Okay..." Sadie said. "I don't get why I care yet."

"Patience, Sadie," Robin chastised, taking a swig of her La Croix. She tipped her head to the side, studying Sadie. "What a beautiful haircut, dear. You must give me the name of your stylist."

"Moooooom," Sadie groaned.

"Right, right. So anyway, this woman, Arlene, is the wife of the stock contractor. And she was talking a lot of gossip about the rodeo, big name dropper she is, and then on green six she said that Cody Clark is leaving the rodeo!"

Arlo gasped.

Sadie frowned.

Luna grunted.

"Why would he leave?" Arlo asked. "He's a hit. Everyone loves him."

"That's why it's so confusing. Arlene was speculating it had something to do with Malcolm. Apparently, there was bad blood between them."

"Arlene implied Cody killed Malcolm because of some bad blood between them and now he's skipping town because of it?" Sadie asked, interested. When she'd opened the door and found Malcolm, Cody had been as shocked as she had been. She didn't think he was that good of an actor.

"That's exactly what she implied," Robin said. "Once I started asking questions, though, she clammed up. I think she realized she'd gone too far."

"Do you know what might have been between Cody and Malcolm, Dad?" Luna's grunting had reached a new pitch, and Sadie was starting to worry about what she was working on. There were only two diapers left in the fanny pack.

Arlo considered. "Malcolm and Cody talked a lot. The only time I can think of them getting into it was last week. Cody was all worked up about something personal, and Malcolm got on his case about being distracted during rehearsal. I thought little of it. For as much as Cody's a clown during performances, he's a quiet guy otherwise."

"Huh. This isn't that convincing, honestly, but I'll talk to Cody."

"You'll need to do it by tonight's rodeo, because it's his last performance," Robin said. She got up from the table and scooped up Luna. "Now, I'm going to play with this baby. You go work."

"Paige left her with me!"

"Mmm, and now we're stealing her from you, aren't we, Luna-Loo?" Robin crooned to Luna, bouncing up and down and gazing at her adoringly.

"Fine," Sadie said. She pulled out her phone and texted Paige that she'd passed off her darling daughter to her parents. No response, so Sadie checked Facebook for the candidate forum Paige had mentioned. She pulled it up just in time to hear Paige eviscerating Wade over his position against Accessory Dwelling Units. She closed the app, grinning. "Sounds like Paige will be a while yet. I'm going to run home and let Tyrone out, then I'll be back to investigating. Let me know if you need me to come get her."

"Have fun, my little Nancy Drew," Arlo said from the sink where he was washing the lunch dishes. "And be careful."

"Always, Dad," Sadie promised, kissing his cheek before leaving out the back door.

Chapter Ten

While Sadie let Tyrone run around the backyard, she checked her phone for messages. Jake had texted her back.

I'm in Oregon with the crew kicking this fire's
ass. Hoping to be home in time for Astrid's
first day. Heard about the thing at the
shootout. Stay safe.

Word certainly traveled fast. She texted him a quick thanks and hopes that he stayed safe, too, then she sent a text to Kendall.

Everything okay after your talk with Claire last
night?

"It's all good," Kendall texted back right away. Phew.

I guess Malcolm was a member at your gym.
Can you ask around about him?

10-4 good buddy

Well, that was sorted. Sadie pulled up Gavin's contact and tried to decide if she should text or call him. He wasn't good about seeing or responding to texts. Finally, she chose a phone call.

"Moose?" He answered, distracted.

"Malcolm liked the fancier restaurants in town. Can you ask around?"

"Come over and taste this sauce I made and sure."

"Now?"

"Now."

"Fine, but I also need a buddy for an investigation later. Want to tag along? Tonight? Say...seven?"

"Whatever, just get your ass over here to taste this sauce."

"You're going to love the rodeo."

Sadie hung up while Gavin protested, grinning. A distracted chef was all too easy of a mark. She couldn't wait to share this slice of Jackson with him. Sadie herded Tyrone back into the house, giving him ear scratches and treats to make up for his forced inside time, then clipped on her bike helmet and headed out the door for her bike. She'd ride over to Carloni's, the restaurant Gavin had taken over from her neighbors when they'd retired. He was reworking it into a homey farm-to-table gastropub worthy of his recently won title of Best Chef on the popular reality series.

Sadie linked onto a bike path a couple of blocks from her house, so it was a quick trip over to the restaurant on the south side of town. It was a squat brick building with a hop-covered deck to one side. Sadie noticed the building next door, a newly constructed modern office building, was for lease. Sadie hoped Gavin got good neighbors.

She entered through the kitchen, which was sparkling clean

and filled with the new appliances Gavin had won as part of his reality show prize winnings. He stood at a stainless-steel prep bench, an array of deli containers filled with interesting concoctions in front of him.

"Took you long enough," he complained.

"I biked," Sadie explained. She stood next to him and examined the containers. "What are you making?"

"I'm working on a puttanesca sauce," he explained.

"Yum." Sadie reached for a tasting spoon, but he stopped her.

"I want you to try it with pasta," he said, gesturing at a pot of boiling water. "Give it a minute and it will be ready."

"I just ate lunch," Sadie protested.

"And you'll eat again if you want me to help you tonight. And really, a rodeo?" Gavin checked the pasta in the water, then pulled it out to strain. Working efficiently, he distributed a small twirl of the fresh spaghetti in another set of deli containers, then ladled sauces from different containers. Sadie watched with fascination.

"Oh, you'll love it," Sadie said, reaching for the first container he offered her. Sadie's mouth watered at the spicy, lemony, tomatoey scent. "Have you ever been to a rodeo?"

"I watched the episode of the Real Housewives of New York when they went to a small-town rodeo in Montana."

Sadie shoveled the first sample of pasta in her mouth, taking a minute to savor it. Salty from the capers, anchovies, and olives. Not in a bad way, but salty enough she wasn't sure she'd be able to finish a whole bowl. She told Gavin as much and he frowned at her, then shoved a glass of sparkling water in her hand.

"Palate cleanse."

Sadie obliged. "So, is that a no, then?"

"It's a no. But I'm always up for new experiences. So, we're going to the rodeo? You really thought you were going to get me on this one, didn't you? Fancy gay TV chef goes to the rodeo and squeals about it?"

"I thought I'd at least get a little squeal," Sadie admitted. The second dish of pasta was more acidic than the first, and she liked the brightness.

"I contain multitudes, Sadie Moose. Which reminds me, I like your haircut."

"Well thank you. And of course you do. So complex. Like this sauce," Sadie said, eyes widening as she tasted the third dish. "Wow. This is the winner. I don't want to taste anything else. What's different about this one?"

"I roasted the capers," he said smugly.

"It's killer." Sadie scraped the sauce off the container with her fork and licked it clean. "Man. I'd come back for that every night."

"Tuesday through Saturday to start," Gavin reminded her. "We're starting this thing slow."

"When do you think you'll open?"

"By Halloween, if I'm lucky," he said, putting lids on the carefully labeled containers. "My front of the house is moving here next month, then we'll start hiring and training. The renovation is moving along on pace."

"Exciting," Sadie said. "I'm so happy for you. Decide on a name yet?"

"I have some ideas," he said cagily. "I'll let you know when I'm ready to workshop them."

"Multitudes, right?" Sadie said, winking at him. "I'm going to go, then. Meet me at my house around six-thirty? Wear your best cowboy clothes and come ready to snoop."

"Speaking of the investigation," he said, stopping her. "I already heard some info about your dead guy."

"That was fast."

"I work in a kitchen. The least I can do is get you information on anyone in this town."

"What's the most you could do?"

"Need anyone killed? I probably know a line cook that will do it. For free."

Sadie laughed, and Gavin joined her.

"You tell funny jokes."

"Right. I was totally joking. Anyway, Malcolm was a generous tipper but picky orderer. He claimed to be allergic to a variety of things that continued to change over time, leading servers to think he was picking things to satisfy his variety of diets and blaming it on allergies. Except for one thing—he was deathly allergic to pepper."

"Yikes. How does one eat out if they're allergic to pepper?"

"Remember that scene in Mrs. Doubtfire when Pierce Brosnan is having an allergic reaction to pepper and Robin Williams has to save him, blowing his cover?"

"Yes?"

"So does everyone else in the food industry. We're serious about that shit."

"Okay. So, he might have had an allergy to pepper. Interesting. According to the police, he died from ingesting a lethal amount of anti-parasite medication."

"Like ivermectin?"

"Why does that sound familiar?"

"Do you remember Covid? Remember anti-vaxxers? When they started coming up with bizarre, dangerous treatments? Drinking bleach? Taking horse medicine?"

"Ohhhhh, right. Wait. Ivermectin is a *horse medicine*?"

"And we're going to a rodeo tonight. Tell me there's not a connection."

"You're a real Columbo, you know that?"

"I'm adding that to my list of potential restaurant names. Now get out of here, I've got to clean."

As Sadie walked through the door, he called her name.

"Yes?" she said.

"Smashing new haircut."

* * *

Sadie was close to the newspaper office, so she stopped in to pester Penny for information. The *Jackson Hole Journal* was housed in a building built in the seventies, blocky and predictable, with a dusty atrium at the entrance. Unlike many small newspapers that had outsourced the printing over the years, the *Journal* still printed in house. Jackson was in a valley surrounded by tall mountains—hence the hole—that experienced frequent road closures in the winter. They had to be self-sufficient to get the paper out every day. That said, the crew was small. Randall was the editor and only full-time reporter. Penny was the office manager, occasional reporter, and ad guru. They worked with a couple of stringers for freelance stories, and the printing press and distribution ran on a skeleton crew. They were such a small operation after years of downsizing and consolidation they'd taken to renting out the extra cubicles to remote workers.

Penny wasn't at her desk, but Sadie followed her voice, which echoed throughout the bullpen, to the break room. She took a minute to absorb today's look before she interrupted Penny's conversation with Randall. Penny had been wearing a lot of pink lately, her "Barbie period" as she called it, and today was no different. She was wearing high-waisted button jeans, hot pink cowboy boots, a ruffly off-the-shoulder pink-and-white gingham blouse, and a straw cowboy hat with a pink hatband.

"Daisy Duke? Is that you?" Sadie asked, and Penny turned with a frown, which immediately turned to a grin.

"Your hair! I love it! Oh my God! It's been the same since you were eleven, Sadie. I'd lost hope you'd ever change it!"

Sadie ran a hand over her shortened hair, pleased. Juliana had definitely been on to something.

"I'm not wearing shorts, though, Sadie, so I'm not Daisy Duke," Penny corrected. "If anything, I'm Cowboy Barbie."

Right, of course. "Cowboy Barbie, you look fantastic. Why are you a cowboy today?"

"Oh, Randall gave me the job of covering the rodeo tonight!"

Sadie glanced at Randall, who looked miserable, his foot in a cast up to his knee. "Why tonight?"

"We haven't really done any coverage of it yet this summer, and despite a murder this week, it's a pretty slow news cycle," Randall explained.

"How exciting," Sadie said. "I'm going too. And Gavin."

"Oh, yay!" Penny said, clapping her hands. "You can come sit with me in VIP."

"Press seating," Randall corrected.

"Right, VIP press seating," Penny agreed. "Now, Randall, I imagine Sadie's here to talk to me, so I'm going to take my break now."

"And that's different from most of your time here how?"

Penny pretended not to hear him, and Sadie waved to him as they left the room, headed for the outdoor courtyard. Penny waved at a few people in cubicles on the way, who seemed nonplussed by her outfit. She supposed if you saw Penny every day, eventually you would be immune to the pageantry. Sadie had known Penny since they were in pre-K together, though, and she was still sometimes stunned to silence.

Once in the courtyard and seated on a hot-to-touch plastic picnic table, Penny dished.

"Okay, so they've narrowed down the delivery of the poison to two things—either someone crammed it down his throat, but since it took over a week for him to die, probably that's not it, or they put it in his vape pen."

"What!?"

"I know, scandalous, right? So, there were traces in his vape pen, but they can't prove that they didn't get in there from contact with his mouth, I guess? But the most likely thing to me seems to be that he *vaped the poison.*"

"Wow. What kind of cartridge does a vape pen take?" Sadie asked.

"What was he vaping?"

"I presume tobacco?" Sadie guessed.

"Well, you can buy refillable cartridges. Maybe he used that kind, and someone got a hold of it. Or messed with his refill container."

"Hmmm...do you know if the cops have tested his refill container?"

"I'll ask Greg," Penny said. "I wonder if he shopped in town?"

"Maybe," Sadie said, adding that to her mental list of things to do. "I saw him take hits of his vape pen that afternoon quite a few times. And Juliana said this morning that he was always using it. So if you wanted to slip him something, that was a good way to do it."

"How devious, though," Penny mused.

"Someone must've been pretty mad," Sadie agreed. "But I feel like this detail might exonerate my dad. He doesn't know his way around a vape pen."

"True," Penny agreed. "But he's a smart man and could figure it out."

"But he has no motive. He didn't hate Malcolm. He was grateful to him for restoring the stagecoach so the act could move forward. It doesn't make any sense. And being the last person to see him alive doesn't mean anything, either, when the method of death could've been over a long period of time."

Penny shrugged. "Regardless, he's still a suspect. Maybe you can convince Will to strike him off the list, though. Perhaps over dinner?" Penny batted her eyes, her fake eyelashes fluttering rapidly, and Sadie stood, waving her off.

"I don't think so. I'll take him to dinner because I owe him one, but I don't think I can date him. It's too blurry, the difference between friend and cop."

"That I get," Penny said soberly. Then she brightened. "I'll tell you once I slept with Greg, I stopped worrying about it. Have you considering sleeping with Will?"

"Penny," Sadie groaned.

"Sadieeeee," Penny groaned back.

"See you at the rodeo," Sadie said, heading for her bike. "Can't wait to sit in VIP with you."

Chapter Eleven

On the way back to her house, she swung by Schultz's Shirts hoping to find Ted Shultz, but the shop was closed, a "back in one hour" sign on the door. Odd. It was midday during high tourism season. Why were they closed? Stymied, Sadie biked home. She spent the rest of the afternoon puttering around the house while she thought about the case. Headphones on, true crime podcast rolling, she scrubbed and cleaned and mopped and organized, all the while wondering: who killed Malcolm Radcliffe?

She went over what she knew.

Malcolm had been showing signs he was unwell at least since the morning of his death, when Vivian confronted him about the lease termination and he was pale and coughing. Sadie had noticed his makeup running that afternoon and Juliana had said she'd had to use extra blush on him to give him some color. He'd been coughing but persisted on using his vape pen, and she'd seen him bump into things and stumble several times. Sadie had guessed he was just getting whatever Amanda was out with, which tickled something in her brain. She needed to check in with Amanda. Was she better? What had she been sick with? That needed to be cleared up before she could chalk up Malcolm's symptoms to the poison.

The show had gone mostly according to script until Malcolm hadn't burst from the coach victorious at the end. Prior to that moment, the last person to see him had been Arlo, as he jumped off the top of the coach. Well, and Cody. But he'd been occupied with driving the coach and keeping the horses calm, so she doubted he'd seen him any later. But how would that matter if Malcolm was already under the influence of the poison? Why had he succumbed at that moment, in the coach, rather than at any other point? Had he taken a hit of his vape pen while he was in there, the last fatal dose?

Sadie straightened from where she was hunched over her dryer, unloading towels. Wait, that actually made sense. In the thirty or so seconds Malcolm had in the coach before he needed to burst out, it did seem like he'd use his vape. And that must've been the dose that led to the cardiac arrest. Whoever had plotted to kill him hadn't known he'd do that, hadn't known he'd die then. They hadn't been able to plan it.

But who had a motive to kill him?

Malcolm had outraged Vivian Benson, but even with him dead, it was possible Teton Tots would still be forced to close if they couldn't find a new lease. Killing Malcolm solved nothing for her, and Sadie had a hard time seeing the intense ultra-marathoner supermom killing in a fit of rage. Plus, poisoning a vape pen with horse medicine? How would she get a hold of either the medicine or Malcolm's vape?

Helen and Bob Foster disliked Malcolm. They thought he had taken away their life's work, shuffled them to the chorus line when they used to be lead performers. But Helen had an alibi, and Bob hadn't been seen at the Playhouse in weeks. When would he have poisoned the vape pen? And where would he have gotten the horse medicine? Plus, while they may have disliked Malcolm, he had brought in the money that improved the Playhouse, and now that was cut off for good. Would they kill him if they thought he had more to give?

And she couldn't forget Ted Shultz. For someone who'd supposedly once been a friend to Malcolm, he hadn't had anything nice to say in the minutes after his death. What had their falling out truly been about, and did Ted still hold a grudge?

And then there was Cody. There were the unverified rumors of bad blood, and she didn't understand what his motive could be, but he had horses, which meant access to horse medicine, and he was around Malcolm often while they rehearsed for the shootout. Plus, he was leaving town unexpectedly. Was that enough for him to be guilty? She'd confront him tonight to find out more.

Speaking of tonight, it was probably time for her to shower and get ready. She shoved the now-folded towels into the hall closet, mind still whirling with case information. A thump at the door interrupted her.

Frowning because she hadn't gotten a notification for motion at her front door on her phone, Sadie walked to it and peeked out the peephole. No one was there. She opened the door warily, looking both directions to make sure no one was hiding around the corner of the house to jump her. Still no one. Had she imagined it? But then she saw the package on the bottom step.

The hair on the back of her neck stood up.

This wasn't an Amazon package.

It was a small brown box.

And the corner of it was dripping with a red liquid.

A liquid that looked like blood.

* * *

Will was apparently out of cell phone service, so dispatch sent his favorite patrol officer, Officer Greg Knott, instead. Sadie had asked if the bomb squad needed to come, but according to their standard operating procedures, small boxes dripping red liquid didn't trigger a bomb squad response.

Which was probably for the best. She did have plans later.

When Greg arrived, he took some official pictures with his iPad, then put on a pair of gloves. "Think you can film while I open it?"

"Sounds like you need a partner, Greg."

"I do," he said earnestly. "I really do. It gets lonely all day out on the streets, you know?"

"Right," Sadie said. "Well, right now, I'm your partner. Hand me that iPad."

Sadie held the iPad steady while Greg carefully cut the taped-down lid to the box open on her step. They both held their breath when he flipped the lid open.

"Ew," Sadie said.

Greg gave her a reproachful look, then said in an official voice for the evidence film, "when opened, the box contains a severed toy horse head covered in what looks to be...strawberry syrup. The liquid is sticky and smells like strawberries."

"Any message?" Sadie asked, peering into the box lid.

"I think it sends a message, don't you? I don't see any words. You can stop filming. To be safe, I'm going to bag this into evidence." Greg took more pictures, then bagged everything. Sadie was still puzzling over the message.

"What's the message?" She asked when Greg was finally done.

He blinked at her. "A severed horse head?"

"Yeah. What does it mean? Someone's going to kill my horse? I don't have a horse."

"It's from the Godfather," Greg said, incredulous. Greg was in his late twenties, a white man with a baby face and a buzz cut who loved sports, domestic beer, Penny, and apparently, cinematic classics.

"Okay...?"

"It can mean a couple things. One, we're gonna make you an offer you can't refuse," Greg said the last part in a dreadful Marlon Brando impression.

"Okay?"

"Or, it can mean...simply, you're dead."

"Oh."

"Yeah. I'd take this seriously. It may be a toy covered in ice cream topping, but someone went through the trouble of getting it here. No footage on your camera?"

Sadie looked away sheepishly. "Battery's dead."

"Classic Sadie," Greg said, sighing. "Regardless, they most likely wore a mask or came from the side of the house or something when they saw you had one. I'll ask around and see if anyone saw anything weird. In the meantime...try to stay out of trouble? Just...do something normal tonight. With friends."

Sadie brightened at that. "Oh, me and Penny and Gavin are going to the rodeo to sit in VIP seats!"

"Great!" Greg said, smiling. "That's super normal. Keep that up."

Sadie kept the part where she was going to question a suspect to herself. That was certainly not normal. But when Greg left, Sadie made sure her door was locked, then double checked every window in the house. She replaced the doorbell camera battery and checked the rest of the security system her dad has installed when she'd been attacked in the alley last fall.

It was in working order, and had recorded nothing suspicious, at least in the last few days.

Still, before she stepped into the shower, she set the security system alarm. Just in case.

* * *

Going to the rodeo with Penny was a gas.

She'd upgraded her outfit, adding a hot pink suede vest affixed with a shiny silver star over the breast and an entire vintage Stetson hatbox on a string for a purse. Tourists stopped her for pictures half a dozen times as they made their way into the stands.

"Are you a rodeo queen?" One little girl asked her during a picture.

Penny had shaken her head. "No, baby, I'm the villain," she'd said. The girl had been delighted.

Sadie had dressed in skinny jeans, ankle boots, and a flannel over a tank top. When the sun finally went down, it would get chilly in the stands. She'd scrunched her hair with the products Juliana had insisted she buy, and she was pleased with the gentle waves in her hair.

Gavin was dressed like a tech bro. Straight jeans, running shoes, a button up and a Patagonia vest. If he added a pair of wire-rimmed glasses she would have called him Zuckerberg. But at the Jackson Hole Rodeo, which ran two nights a week from Memorial Day to Labor Day and catered to tourists looking for the true Wild West experience, he fit in just fine. Though most tourists didn't complain as much as he did.

"Hot dogs and hamburgers? For real?" He was frowning at the menu at the concession stand. "Nachos with the nacho cheese cup on the side? What the fuck is a walking taco?"

"A western delicacy," Sadie assured him, stepping up to

order three of them. As the high schooler in the kitchen started preparing the 'taco' by slicing open a package of Fritos with scissors, Gavin quieted, watching with interest.

"Genius," he said, watching the teenager fill the bag with toppings. Sadie paid and Gavin collected the tacos, his mind obviously elsewhere as they made their way behind the chutes to the VIP seating where Penny awaited them, drinks in hand.

"What are you thinking about, Mister Chef?" Sadie asked.

"What else could I make like this? Salmon en papillote? Cut open the side and add toppings to make it 'walking'?"

Sadie liked this game. She played it with bakery ideas all the time. "A bag of pork rinds with pulled pork, jalapeños..."

Gavin stared at her. "Where do you keep the ideas in your brain? Your head should be bigger."

Sadie winked at him, taking two of the bags from his hands and gesturing at the fork stuck in the bag he still held. "If you think the idea is genius, then you should try the reality of it." They showed their VIP passes to the cowboy-hatted guy at the gate and he let them through. Penny spotted them, standing up and waving three aluminum bottles of Bud Light.

"Booze! I got booze!"

"That's...not booze, Penny," Sadie assured her, taking the bottle with a wrinkled nose. Gavin had a point about the quality of food at the rodeo. Would it kill them to have something a little more local? A little more Jackson Hole? They should get the brewpub's traveling beer trailer here on rodeo nights and serve real beer. Then she started feeling bad about being a snob, and she dashed the thought from her mind.

"How is this so good?" Gavin was muttering to himself, shoving another bite of Fritos, ground beef taco meat, beans, sour cream, lettuce, chopped tomato, and hot sauce into his mouth. "It shouldn't be this good."

"I think you broke his brain," Penny hiss-whispered at her,

and they both giggled while they settled into their seats. The VIP area was otherwise empty, but Sadie imagined more people would trickle in as the events got started. Rodeos usually started with the bareback riding event and ended with the bull riding, which kept everyone excited and in their seats until the end.

Sadie felt her pocket buzz and pulled her phone out. She had three text messages.

From Kendall:

> *Malcolm came to the gym regularly. Cardio rat. Liked spin class. Known to whine a lot but post on Instagram how awesome he was. He last came in on Monday and people noticed he was more gassed than usual, and pale. Thought he might be getting sick.*

From Paige:

> *Thanks for taking Luna earlier! Warning: I could barely pry her from your parent's paws. I think their grandparent clocks are ticking or whatever. Kicked Wade's ass today. Canvass with me this weekend?*

From Will:

> *For the love of Pokémon Sadie stop poking around in things you're going to end up hurt. I don't know why—*

Sadie sighed and turned her phone screen off, refusing to read the rest of Will's message. Why, when she was investigating, did *she* always get blamed for threats on her life instead of the people that were making the threats?

Gavin stood suddenly. "I'm going to get another one," he declared. "I think a simple ratio change could vastly improve the quality of the 'walking taco', so don't expect me back for a while I get them sorted out."

Sadie winced as he walked away. "He's going to get us kicked out of here."

"Probably," Penny said, taking a swig of her beer. "But at least I'll have something to write about."

Chapter Twelve

O ver the course of the run up to the first event, the VIP section started to fill. By the time the real rodeo queen had taken laps while holding the American flag, a poem about Old Glory being read in a nostalgic tone from the western-twanged announcer, it was almost full. Sadie peered around to see who she knew. Most people in the crowd were either tourists that had big bucks to spend on the good tickets or locals who were sponsors and had comped tickets. Because of that, she didn't recognize many people, but she did see Wade Fisher a few rows away. Was it her imagination, or did he look a little shellshocked? Paige could do that to a person in her cool, mindful way. Good for her.

She was a little surprised to see Vivian Benson with her family, but when she mentioned it to Penny, she found out Vivian's husband was the manager at the runner's store, who was a sponsor. Helen and Bob Foster were also there. They both steadfastly avoided her gaze. And Ted Shultz was there with a petite older blonde woman, probably his wife, Tiffany, who she didn't recall ever meeting. Shultz's Shirts was one of the chute sponsors, so she wasn't surprised to see them. Sadie wondered why their store had been closed earlier. Likely just a staffing problem. It was hard to hold on to workers in a town where housing was almost impossible to find. Plus, the college students were headed back to college this month. Maybe she could corner him during the rodeo to ask him her questions.

"It's interesting that so many of my suspects are here," Sadie whispered to Penny once the Star-Spangled Banner was over and the first event was starting.

"Oooh, dish," Penny said. She'd bought a bag of kettle corn from a wandering vendor and was tossing pieces in the air to catch them to the disconcert of the people in the row behind them.

Sadie quietly filled her in on her theories, which Penny considered noisily.

"Well, Vivian has kids, so she probably has access to toy horses," she said after contemplation, and Sadie elbowed her.

"Not so loud," she hissed. The crowd erupted around them as a cowboy stayed on his bucking bronc for the full eight seconds, and Penny looked around, mystified.

"Why does everyone cheer for the cowboy?" She asked. "I always cheer for the animal."

"Of course you do. I wasn't going to bring up the whole horse in a box thing tonight, but I should've guessed Greg told you."

"He sent me a picture even."

"So much for police confidentiality."

"I'm really, really good in bed."

"I'm going to need another drink if this is how you are all night. Beer me, beer man!" Sadie called to a nearby vendor, Penny chuckling beside her.

Gavin returned with another walking taco, a smug look on his face. "The high school rodeo team will now be making a full dollar more per taco thanks to my tutelage on food costs, and the ratio is much better," he boasted.

"You're a civil servant at heart, Gavin," Sadie said, squeezing his arm, and he winked at her. His tough chef persona was an act. He'd once ran to the edge of a crumbling cliff with her to save three strangers caught in a landslide. They'd risked their lives, together, to save them, while a gaggle of others from much higher tax brackets gasped and clutched their expensive diamonds to their throats in shock. That experience, along with a murder and surviving that together, had bonded them for life.

"Wait, why doesn't that horse have a saddle on?" He asked, squinting at the arena.

Sadie explained the varied events to him, and he joined Penny in rooting for the animals throughout the bareback riding and the steer wrestling, which he mostly covered his eyes for.

"Aren't you a butcher?" Sadie asked him.

"Yes, but I only wrestle *dead animals*," he said from behind his hands.

Penny and Gavin's strategy failed them during the tie down roping.

"I want to root for the horse in this case," Penny said, frowning. "They seem to be doing the most important job holding the rope taut like that. Look at how focused they are. What good good horses."

"Agreed." Gavin frowned. "How about this: I'll root for the steers, you root for the horses?"

This continued throughout the team roping, where much gnashing of teeth over which horse was prettier and a gooder gooder horse ensued. They entertained Sadie if nothing else. Then came an intermission announcement, which caught her attention.

"Folks, you're going to want to stay in your seats for this

one. For over five summers now, Cody Carter has been working this rodeo. You've seen him at the National Finals Rodeo as a bullfighter. You've seen him in the PRCA Extreme Bulls competitions, but he always comes back to Jackson in the summer. But tonight, sad news, folks, is his last night." The crowd moaned in sadness. "Stick around with us as Cody performs during intermission for the last time, and you won't want to miss him during the bull riding tonight. I saw those bulls out in the pen and let me tell you they are meaaaannnnnn!" The crowd roared, their earlier sadness forgotten.

"I understood about thirty percent of that," Gavin mused from beside her.

"Shush," Sadie said, sitting forward to watch as Cody came out to perform his clown routine. He had several assistants with him, and Sadie noticed with interest that they were all from the shootout. Amanda was there, apparently well again and not dressed in orange satin, but oversized overalls with a daisy on the front Sadie guessed squirted water. The three robbers were there, too, as indistinguishable to her as they'd been before, all white, tall, and bearded with scruffy hair. Arlo hadn't mentioned that they all worked together in this show, too. Interesting.

The act was brief but funny and featured trick roping and yes, water squirting out of the flower at just the right moment. When it ended, people filtered out of the stands to get refreshments and more walking tacos, but Sadie snuck out before all of them. She'd seen where the cast entered the arena, and she wanted to catch them before they dispersed.

* * *

Darkness had fallen, but the arena lights lit up the night. Sadie found a shadow to hide in, waiting for Cody and his crew to walk by her before she stepped into their path.

"Woah," Amanda said, her hand over her heart. "You scared the shit out of me, lady."

"Sadie," Cody said. "Good to see you." He was tall, leanly built white man with curly blonde hair that spilled out from under his tan cowboy hat.

Amanda was white, a couple inches taller than Sadie, with brown hair and blue eyes. She took a second look at Sadie. "This is Sadie?" She softened. "I heard you did well on Tuesday. I'm sorry you were in my place to have what happened happen."

That was kind of her. "I appreciate it," Sadie said. "I'm actually glad I ran into y'all, I wanted to ask you a few questions." The three robbers looked around, bored. "You guys, too," Sadie clarified.

Cody hesitated, but finally nodded. "Let's go over by my trailer. I have to change for the bull riding."

The parking lot outside the arena was a sea of trailers, some fancier than others, most a combination horse trailer and living trailer. While they made their way to Cody's, Sadie finally made introductions to the three men.

Ed, to her surprise, had a British accent. He was the robber with no lines except whooping and hollering that had held up Cody. He was in Jackson for the summer before returning to college in South Dakota.

Kaleb was a local kid she realized she knew from high school theater productions. He worked at his parent's gas station when he wasn't at the Playhouse.

Jordan was the robber she'd knocked over the head with the Pikachu backpack, the oldest of the group. He was a bum-about-Jackson type, doing everything from guiding with a local outfitter to running raft trips to ski instructing to working at a bar to landscaping to earn a living in a town that was notorious for being unable to live in.

Amanda was from Pinedale, a town two hours to the southeast, and had a degree in stage production, where her true interests were. Playing the busty saloon girl was her way of getting her foot in the door.

Of all of them, Cody was the quietest. When he disappeared inside his trailer to change, Sadie turned the conversation around to ask them some questions.

"Amanda, what were you sick with?"

A twenty-four-hour stomach bug her roommate had too.

"Did any of y'all notice anything going on with Malcolm on Tuesday?"

Ed had noticed Malcolm was tenser than usual and had seen him stumble during their morning rehearsal. Kaleb hadn't noticed anything unusual, but from the scent of pot on his clothes, she had a feeling he might not notice much sometimes. Jordan had noticed Malcolm had flubbed some lines and been a little sluggish in his choreography, but had thought little of it. He'd been the robber that fell off the carriage before Arlo and Malcolm and hadn't seen anything weird.

While they were talking, Kaleb pulled out a vape pen to breathe deeply from it.

"Oh, did you and Malcolm shop at the same store for that? Where do you even go in town?"

Kaleb blinked at her, then at the device in his hand.

"Oh, we both shop at the vape store in the mini mall over by the Dairy Queen," he said after a long pause.

"Cool," Sadie said, adding that to her mental list of places to check out. "Last question. Can you think of anyone that would've wanted to hurt Malcolm?"

"Are you like a detective or something?" Amanda asked, her

eyes lighting up. "You're like Mabel in Only Murders in the Building!"

That was one Sadie hadn't gotten before, but she'd take being compared to Selena Gomez any day. "I'm just nosy, honestly. And looking out for my dad. The police named Arlo as a suspect since he was the last to see Malcolm."

"That's ridiculous," Ed said in his clipped, nasally tone. "Arlo wouldn't hurt a fly."

"I know that as well as y'all," Sadie agreed. "Hence why I'm asking questions."

"So cool," Amanda gushed. There was a long pause while they thought about her question.

"I mean, Helen and Bob hate Malcolm," Kaleb finally said. "They don't even try to hide it."

"I've heard that about them," Sadie hedged.

"With him gone, they won't have as much money to play with, but Bob will get his favorite parts back and Helen will be able to make her own calls again," Amanda said sagely. "They had a lot to gain from his death. But don't tell them I said that, okay? I don't want to get fired!"

Sadie mimed locking her mouth and throwing away the key. "All secrets are safe with me," she promised.

Cody exited his trailer and joined their group then, dressed in oversized shorts held up by suspenders and covered in neon flags. Underneath the baggy shirt he wore, Sadie knew he wore a vest to protect him from errant horns or being crushed beneath the weight of an angry 1,500-plus-pound bull.

The announcer was calling everyone back before the saddle bronc started, and Cody winced. "I gotta go," he said. "I know we didn't get a chance to talk." He looked at the group, then pulled Sadie to the side, looking at her earnestly under his clown makeup and the brim of his cowboy hat. "I want to talk to you about something important, though. I know you're looking into this on behalf of Arlo. I have something I want to tell you about Malcolm. Meet me here after the show? I'm headed out of town as soon as I can get packed up, but I should have time to talk."

Sadie wanted to know what he knew now, but she could tell from the way he kept glancing at the arena lights he really had to go. Fine. She could be patient.

"Go," she said. "I'll see you after the show. And be careful."

He tipped his hat at her and ran off.

Amanda and the three guys walked back to VIP with her, flashing their own passes they got thanks to being part of the performance. "It's our last night," Amanda moped. "They're calling up some other clown to take Cody's place, and he prob-ably doesn't need us for his act."

"Are rodeo clowns always men?" Sadie asked as they made their way to their seats. Penny's behavior had cleared out a big enough section around them her new friends could join them no problem.

That question incited a round of Googling that led them all into the saddle bronc after Sadie made introductions, and then the barrel racing. Penny was more than half lit from the three Bud Lights she'd drank and spent the entire event rating the rider's flashy clothing to the raucous delight of the actors.

Then it was time for the bull riding. The atmosphere got heavy, the music low and drumming. The audience, half drunk and completely riled up from a night of high scores and wild rides, hit a fever pitch as the first bull burst out of the chute, immediately bouncing its rider high into the sky and aiming straight for the falling body before being distracted by Cody.

Gavin gripped her arm, white-faced, while the fallen cowboy hustled out of the arena. Sadie patted his hand. "There's a reason they save it for last," Sadie told him.

"Long live cowboys," he breathed.

"Amen," Penny whooped.

"Hallelujah," Amanda answered.

The night was cool, the lights were bright, and the cowboys looked great in their Wranglers. Altogether, it was a great night, murder, threats, and secrets aside.

Chapter Thirteen

P enny begged off going to question Cody after getting a text from Greg that made her blush, but Gavin agreed to go along with Sadie. That made Sadie more comfortable. While there were people all around as the rodeo let out, she couldn't help but feel a little weird outside, alone in the dark after the warning she'd received hours before.

What was the message? That she was being offered a deal she couldn't refuse? Like what? Or that...she was dead if she kept asking questions? Sadie shivered in her flannel, again glad that Gavin was with her. She'd find out what Cody knew, then go home and take a hot shower before falling into bed. That would take the chill away.

"I forgot until now," Gavin said as they walked the rows of trailers where people in western wear bustled about packing things up. "I heard the same thing from a couple of different servers. Apparently Malcolm always used an AMEX black card, but it had a different name on it."

"Like a company name?"

"No. Mike Smith."

"That's...bizarre. Okay. Some sort of alias? Or was Malcolm a stage name? But his dad's a Radcliffe."

"I knew that would stump ya. I believe you'll figure it out, though, my little sleuth. Maybe that's what Cody wants to talk to you about."

But when they got to Cody's trailer, he wasn't there. A horse was tethered to the back of the trailer, but he was nowhere to be seen.

"Huh," Sadie said. "He said he'd be here."

"He could be held up somewhere." Gavin shrugged. "Introduce me to a horse?"

Sadie rolled her eyes, but she showed Gavin how to approach the horse and not get kicked. Soon, Gavin was crooning over how soft the buckskin's nose was.

"I could forget the restaurant and use that prize money to buy horses," he said suddenly. "I'd look great in those tight jeans."

"A fully staffed kitchen is probably somehow less work," Sadie laughed. "You have no idea."

"You're right," Gavin said, sighing.

Sadie wandered around the side of the trailer, looking back towards the arena. She didn't see Cody coming, and trailers were starting to load out already. Maybe he was just collecting his last paycheck?

A soft moan drew her attention, and suddenly she gasped. There was a booted foot laying on the ground in front of her.

"Gavin!" She cried, running forward and seeing that the foot was attached to Cody's limp body. Blood was pooling in the dirt underneath his head. She heard Gavin run up behind her.

"Shit!" He said. "I'll call 911."

Sadie tore off her flannel and knelt, shoving it against Cody's head wound, trying not to jostle him as she stemmed the flow of blood.

"Cody!" she shouted at him. "Cody, wake up!" She could hear Gavin on the phone with 911. During the rodeo, there was always an ambulance on site. Sadie hoped they were still at the arena. Cody didn't react to her yells. Had she actually heard him moan? She used one hand to check for a pulse and was grateful to feel one. It was weak, but it was there. She pressed more firmly on his head wound, her own heart racing.

What had happened to him?

Had his horse...kicked him in the head? That was not entirely uncommon, but Sadie wouldn't expect a seasoned cowboy like Cody to spook his own horse walking up behind them. Plus, his body wasn't in the right position for that to have happened unless he stumbled a long way, and a quick glance didn't show a blood trail from that direction.

No, whatever had happened to Cody happened right there. There were boot prints in the dirt nearby. Did that show a struggle?

Sadie heard more running feet, and then sirens, and then paramedics were there with her, and Gavin was gently pulling her away. Thank goodness they'd still been on site. They could help him. Surely they could help him.

Gavin pulled her to the other side of the trailer, walking a wide berth around the now-distressed horse. He pulled off his vest and put it on her, then wrapped her in a hug. Sadie realized she was shaking, her teeth chattering.

"Deep breath for me, Sadie," Gavin said. His voice was calm, but Sadie understood the subtext. He had anxiety, too. She'd talked him through a panic attack at the chalet when they'd survived the landslide. He'd talked her through one when he'd been her roommate. She was spiraling and needed to take some action to pull it together.

She let Gavin lead her through box breaths and felt her heartbeat slowing. She was still buzzing with adrenaline and her teeth were chattering, but she wasn't going to need the paramedics, at least.

Red and blue lights flashed against the white of the trailer, and Sadie looked up to see a black SUV pull up nearby. She sighed. Of course it was Detective Will Nolan.

*	*	*

Gavin and Sadie were walked back to the arena by a stern-faced patrol officer Sadie didn't recognize, then asked to wait in the ticket office until they could be interviewed. The ambulance had taken off with Cody inside, and Sadie hoped he was okay. She didn't know him well, and had every reason to believe he might be involved in Malcolm's murder, but she didn't want him to be injured grievously. She thought back to his tone of voice earlier when he'd told her he had something to tell her. It'd been earnest, and a little scared. Sadie had the impression he'd thought telling her what he knew might help him, and she felt guilty she hadn't made it in time to get the information. What could he possibly know about Malcolm? Had that information been what got him bashed over the head?

Gavin paced in the small office while Sadie sat, thinking. She pulled out her phone and opened Facebook, navigating to Malcolm's profile again. There'd been no posts from anyone expressing their grief, but that could just be his privacy settings. She looked at his friend list, scrolling through. Cody wasn't on it. Neither was anyone with the last name of Smith. She looked up Cody's profile, going through his about info. A detail immediately popped out at her.

Cody's hometown was listed as Gilroy, California.

Which was the same place Malcolm had grown up.

Cody was at least a decade younger than Malcolm, though. Was it possible they knew each other from their hometown?

Gilroy wasn't exactly tiny, but it wasn't a metropolis of millions, either. It was possible they'd gone to the same schools, or had siblings in each other's classes, despite the age difference. Cody's parents could have known Malcolm's. And if they were both involved in the acting scene, that made it even more likely they might know each other.

Had Malcolm known something Cody didn't want anyone else to know? She hadn't understood what his motive to kill Malcolm could've been, but it was an intriguing idea.

But now Cody had a probable traumatic brain injury and was headed to the hospital, unconscious. If he'd killed Malcolm, who'd gone after him?

It was clear to Sadie she needed to do more digging on Malcolm and Cody's backgrounds. And who was Mike Smith? Whatever they were involved in, it was possible it had all started somewhere else entirely, and was just playing out on the streets of Jackson Hole.

The door to the ticket office opened, and Will motioned for them to exit. Her and Gavin stood against the wall while he studied them.

"Cody woke up in the ambulance," he said after a moment. "He immediately passed back out and I understand the doctors might keep him under to help him heal, but he's alive, at least. Thanks to your finding him so quickly."

"Phew," Sadie sagged against the wall in relief.

"His wallet was still in his pocket, including a wad of cash he'd received as a goodbye bonus tonight. As far as we can tell, nothing was taken from his trailer, which was locked. This wasn't a robbery."

"Who would've done this to him?"

Will's jaw tightened. "That's for us, the police, to figure out, Sadie."

"Weird," Sadie snapped. "Last night you were on my back

deck drinking wine and discussing case details with me, encouraging me, telling me you didn't want me to stop poking around because I was good at it. That's over now?"

"Uh oh," Gavin said under his breath. He looked around. "Can I go?"

Will glowered at him, but finally, he nodded. "An officer will take your statement in the arena, and then you can go. That's where we've gathered everyone we want to question."

"Great," Gavin sighed. "I'll go wait there. Sadie, I'll walk you home when it's time, okay?"

"I'll take her home," Will said, his voice steely.

Gavin didn't move, waiting for Sadie to confirm that was okay.

"Yeah, it's okay, Gavin. Will can take me home when this is over."

"Okay. Call me tomorrow."

"Yep."

When he walked away, they were alone.

Sadie was the one to break the silence. "Why, when bad things happen, do you blame me for them? I didn't send myself a threatening text message or box with a horse head in it. I didn't bash Cody over the head. I didn't do any of these things. Why not blame the perpetrator instead of getting angry with me?"

"You got a threatening text message?" Will's gaze sharpened.

Sadie winced. Right. She hadn't mentioned that to him. Or anyone.

"Last night." Sadie pulled it up and showed it to him. He frowned at it. "The number is fake." He took a screenshot of it on her phone and texted it to himself, and then handed the phone back to her.

"I'm sorry," he said after a pause. "I'm stressed about this case, about Jaden being home with a babysitter when he's supposed to be having his summer visit with me, about you being involved in this and maybe getting hurt."

"Don't take your stress out on me," Sadie said simply. She put a hand on his arm. "I appreciate you being worried about me, but when I see you, I don't want to feel dread in my stomach because I know I'm about to get a talking to. Especially when I've just gone through something."

"That's...not what I want you to feel when you see me," he said, stepping closer. He was in her space, too close for Sadie to imagine he'd done it on accident. She could feel the warmth of his body, almost about to brush hers. If she leaned forward the barest inch, she'd press up against him. She wondered what he felt like. He was tall, with a rangy but hard build. If she let herself lean on him, he'd be able to tuck his chin on the top of her head. She bet that would feel nice. That it would feel comforting.

"How do you feel...when you see me?" He asked, his voice a whisper. His piercing blue eyes bore into her, and she felt like he could tell what she felt even when she couldn't.

She swallowed hard, forcing her body to not sway into his heat. Her bare arms were cold, covered in gooseflesh. "Confused," she answered before she could second guess herself. Who could lie to this man? Wasn't that why he was so good at his job?

He smirked. "I'm not sure if that's good or bad." He leaned in closer, brushing his lips against her jawline. "Maybe this will help you be less confused."

And then he kissed her.

It wasn't a soft hello kiss. Not a hi, this is the first time I'm kissing you kiss. No. It was a searing, I want to change your mind about me kiss. It made Sadie's toes curl in her boots, made her lose her breath, made her lose her mind just a little bit as she wrapped her arms around his neck and pulled him up against her, learning what his hard body felt like against her soft one. It was a kiss where after just a moment, his hands were on her ass, pulling her against him. It was—not a kiss one should have in public during an active crime scene investigation, turns out.

"Hey Nolan, do you want me to start—oooh, never mind," a voice said from behind Will, and Sadie stiffened, pushing Will away from her. "I'll, uh...start statements now." Footsteps hurried away from them.

Awkward.

Will blew out a long breath, holding onto the back of his neck and looking behind him at the retreating officer.

Sadie bit back an inappropriate laugh. Busted.

"Nothing about this is funny," Will reproached, but his voice hinted at his own amusement.

"Absolutely. Not. Funny," Sadie agreed, putting her hand over her mouth to hold in a giggle.

"Okay," he said. "I'm going to walk you home now. I'm going to keep my hands to myself. You're going to give me your statement. Then you're going to lock yourself in your house and stay safe until the morning. Got it?"

Sadie didn't think she liked being bossed around. Correction, she *knew* she didn't like to be bossed around. And yet... something about Will made her kind of like it. Confused. She was still confused. But she let herself be led away from the rodeo grounds, back to her house a few blocks away, and did exactly what Will had directed.

Until she didn't.

Chapter Fourteen

Sadie had every intention of locking herself into her house, taking a long hot shower, then passing out until her alarm blared at the wholly unnatural hour of six in the morning so she could head to the bakery to get an early start on the custom orders that were due for the weekend. She'd even taken off her boots and jeans and had started the shower. She was settling in.

But then KitKat came calling.

She was in her bedroom when she heard the scratch at her window. She jumped, heart racing, certain the killer was here to get her for real this time. Tyrone exploded into barking protector mode, jumping at the window.

And then Sadie saw the faces grinning at her through it.

She stalked over and unlocked the window, opening it to Kendall and Kamari's giggles. Tyrone saw who it was and settled into his bed.

"What?" she asked.

"Come out with us!" They said in unison. It was clear they'd either already been out or had been pre-gaming downstairs in Kamari's apartment for some time.

"It's almost midnight! On a Thursday! I have to work tomorrow." She narrowed her eyes at them. "And so do you."

"C'mon, Moose! We're young! I mean, you're still young-ish, but we're definitely young. The bars are just now getting going. You need some decompression after the night you've had. We'll have you home before last call, promise." Kendall put her hands under her chin and batted her eyes.

"We need to take that new haircut out on the town, girl!" Kamari cajoled.

"I promised a certain detective I would stay home and stay safe tonight."

Kendall dropped the cutesy act and leaned in close. "Then there's no better place to be than with me and Kamari. We got you. I'll sleep on your couch if you want afterwards."

"With me in the basement, you've got nothing to worry about," Kamari agreed. She held up her arm to show off her muscles, and Kendall did the same, laughing.

They hadn't even asked her what she needed protected from, which meant they somehow knew everything.

"Okay, fine," Sadie sighed. "Give me five minutes and meet me at the front door."

"Yessssss!" KitKat high fived.

* * *

The first bar they took Sadie to was one she didn't even know existed. They entered through a back-alley door guarded by a barrel-chested man in a Batman hoodie who exchanged a complicated handshake with Kendall before letting them in. Sadie was unsure if the handshake was a password or just a show of friendship, but she had little time to worry about it. After going downstairs and through a few twisty hallways, the basement opened into a huge room with laser lights flashing and bass-heavy music reverberating off the concrete walls. The dance floor was a crush of bodies that KitKat pulled her right into the middle of.

Sadie let herself let go.

There was only the beat, only the movement of her body to the music she didn't recognize but that lived in her bones now. As sweat poured down her face, she let go of the anxiety over the case. She let go of the fear she'd felt when she'd seen Cody laying on the cold ground, blood pouring from his head, hat knocked askew. She let go of the confusion of the relationship between her and Will, the heat of the kiss they'd shared, the awkwardness of afterwards. She let go of her worries about her business, her employees, her life. It was just her, Kamari, Kendall, a hundred or so other people, and the music.

After a time, KitKat pulled her off the dance floor and into a quieter back room. Kendall appeared at the booth they'd claimed with drinks, and they all guzzled water before sucking down the vodka and soda with limes she'd brought them.

"So for real, how was your talk with Claire last night?" Sadie asked Kendall.

Kendall grinned. "It really was good. She was worried all the ideas I have for the wedding are somehow me trying to put it off, not that my ADHD loves possibilities, and this is the best hyper focus project I have going right now."

"So did y'all figure out what you're going to do?"

"Nope. She's going to let me spin for a while longer."

"She loves you."

"It's sickening how much, really," Kamari agreed, sighing into her drink.

"I take it your love life isn't going great then," Sadie said.

"It's nonexistent," Kamari complained. "Between workouts, work, babysitting Kendall, and promo for the movie, I'm too busy. Plus, there's just zero prospects."

"Small town problems," Sadie sighed.

"Oh, give me a break, girl. You're pulling more than all of us. First Merritt, then Jake, and now you're smooching Will Nolan at the rodeo ticket office?"

Sadie blushed. "How on earth did you hear about that?"

Kendall raised her hand. "I told her."

"I don't even want to know how you know," Sadie laughed. "Tell me more of your ill-gained knowledge."

"Well...Cody's at the hospital in a medically induced coma while they figure out the extent of his head injury," Kendall said. Sadie had heard about as much from Will.

"It's good you found him when you did," Kamari said, putting her hand on Sadie's and squeezing it. "How are you holding up?"

Sadie shrugged. "I can't put any of these pieces together. Cody wanted to tell me something, but got attacked before he could. I was snooping around on social media, and it turns out they both grew up in the same small town in California. Is it something to do with the past, not the present, that's driving this?"

"At least this should take the attention of Arlo, right? He was home with your mom tonight, I'm sure, nowhere near Cody."

"It should," Sadie agreed. And with him out of the spotlight, now would be the perfect time to step out of the middle of things. But she remembered the fear in Cody's voice, the blood soaking her flannel, and knew she wouldn't.

"I was going to tell you this tomorrow," Kamari began, twirling her straw in her drink, "but I overheard something up in town today. I was eating lunch at D.O.G. and there was a group of realtor-types at one of the tables behind me."

"Lunch or brunch?" Kendall clarified.

"Brunch, obviously," Kamari acceded. "If I'm going to hit D.O.G. I'm getting the Local Spicy."

Sadie's mouth watered at the thought of the famed breakfast burrito. Crispy hash browns, spicy jalapeños, your choice of meat cooked with eggs and cheese on a griddle, and the whole thing wrapped in foil and made to go. She might have to hit them up tomorrow.

"Anyway," Kamari said. "They were talking about Malcolm. Apparently he leased the condo he lived in, it wasn't owned, and... he was behind on his rent to his property management company."

"What?" That shocked Sadie. "But he was super rich!"

"Was he?" Kamari asked. "Or did he just *seem* super rich? Maybe daddy shut off the flow of cash."

"He'd just bought the building that houses Teton Tots next door. He couldn't do that without cash."

Kamari twirled one of her braids around her finger, thinking. "Not sure about that. He could have been the figurehead, you know?"

"Gavin told me that the credit card he used was actually under the name Mike Smith, not Malcolm Radcliffe. I didn't ask Will about it, but there's no way they don't know that. The cops would definitely know all this information. They have access to his legal records, his house, his bank accounts, all that jazz."

"But their lead detective is so distracted because he's head over heels for the mouthy town baker," Kendall teased, and Sadie rolled her eyes. "Okay," Kendall said, hopping up. "Let's go somewhere else."

"It's after one!" Sadie protested.

"And you said we had you until closing time." Kamari linked her arm through Sadie's. "You're already out. We'll pick somewhere quieter this time."

Sadie heard it for the lie it was, but she let them lead her back through the dance floor and out of the basement into the cool night air and to another bar down the street. Because she felt grateful to have friends that cared about her, that helped her, and that knew when she shouldn't be home alone. Even if she was going to have a heckuva hangover the next day.

Chapter Fifteen

Sadie snuck into the back door of the bakery a few minutes before nine, sunglasses covering her bloodshot eyes, her fancy new hair pulled into a messy topknot. She'd downed a half a pot of coffee, a water, a blue Gatorade, 800 milligrams of ibuprofen and a Local Spicy burrito from D.O.G., but she still felt like hell. Why was going out in your thirties so much different from going out in your twenties? In her partying years, she used to stay out until closing time, head to an after party, stumble home around four, and still be up to bake at six. Now she knew she wouldn't be okay for days, and she hadn't even drunk much. It was the lack of sleep that was killing her.

As soon as her bakery staff saw her, they started clapping.

"Sadie Moose, everyone!" Max called, and a few patrons through the pass through started clapping, too. Sadie flipped off her staff, waved through the pass through, and headed straight to her office. She was only two hours late. Maybe she had time to rest her head on her desk, just for a bit.

Fifteen minutes later, a sharp knock at the office door woke her. It was Sage with a to-go cup of coffee and a list in her hand.

"Oh, poor Sadie," she soothed, setting the cup in front of her. "KitKat did you dirty."

"I should know better," Sadie sighed.

"Yep," Sage agreed. "But, bonus for you, you hire amazing people, and Max and I completed all the custom orders already. So you can go home and sleep."

"Seriously?" Sadie snatched the paper from her hand, running through the list of orders and the checkmarks next to them. "How?"

"Kendall texted me at three in the morning and told me if I came in at four, you'd pay double overtime, and...I brought Max with me because...they were with me?" Sage was blushing.

Sadie resisted the urge to pump her fist in the air. She'd been totally right that something was going on between Sage and Max. "Oh," Sadie said, keeping her tone light. "How convenient."

Sage giggled, and Sadie winked. "Well, thank goodness for Kendall because I didn't have that genius idea, and thank goodness for you for coming in and doing it. You didn't have to."

"Mmm, but you know, with inflation, art supplies have gotten more expensive, so I can use the money. And you deserve a night out now and then."

"Do you want me to come back and let you two off early?"

"Nope," Sage said. "Rachael is coming in this afternoon, so she'll help us close. You've got the whole day off, and Max and I are splitting the weekend, so you could make it an entire weekend away. Use it wisely."

Sadie winced. "Such pressure. I'll be in tomorrow morning anyway but thank you. Really. Thank you."

She thanked Max on the way out as well, and then slipped back out the door, coffee in hand. Her investigation list was a half mile long. She needed to talk to Ted Shultz, poke around his shop, go to the vape store, talk to Vivian Benson again, figure out who Mike Smith was, check on Cody, talk to Bob and Helen Foster, poke around the Playhouse...but she wasn't going to be good for anything if she didn't get some rest. First, a nap. She guiltily tossed the cup of coffee into a nearby trash can. No more caffeine for her. Once she woke up, she'd eat a good meal, then set out to investigate.

She had such good intentions.

But she never got her nap.

A block from her house, she got a text from Penny.

Get to the hospital now. Cops arresting Cody soon. Heard he's a little bit awake. Maybe you can talk to him first.

* * *

The hospital was only a half mile away, but a one block deviation would take her to her house, so she stopped by to grab her bike instead of running the whole way. She thought her odds of getting in to talk to Cody were slim. He probably had an officer guarding his door if they hadn't already placed him into custody. The news that he was talking was good. But why were they convinced he had killed Malcolm?

Sadie didn't hear any sirens on the quick bike ride to the hospital, but there was a police cruiser parked outside the entrance. *Dangit.* But she was there. No use in not still trying.

She parked and locked her bike and then went inside, slipping her sunglasses onto her head so she could see. The first trick would be to get past the reception desk, and she'd already goofed it up by standing still and letting her eyes adjust. The friendly woman in a pink coat at the desk smiled at her and offered her a snack from the bin always kept on the counter.

The hospital loved giving out snacks. Sadie didn't get it, but she wasn't one to refuse. She took an apple.

"How can I help you?" The woman asked. She looked concerned at Sadie's haggard appearance. How flattering.

Sadie had to play this carefully. "Um, I'm here to see Hector Sanchez?"

Hector was her favorite nurse, and he'd helped her in the past, though never with anything as devious as what she was going to ask of him today.

"Oh. Does he know you're coming, dear?" She was tapping away at her keyboard, eyes on the screen, probably making sure Hector was on the schedule that day.

"Yes..." Sadie tried hard to sound confident.

"Excellent. I'll page him and let him know to come get you."

This could go horribly wrong.

But it didn't. Within minutes, Hector appeared, smiling like he'd expected her. "Sadie, thank you so much for coming," he said, linking his arm through hers. "Thanks, Brenda," he said to the woman at the desk. "I'll take you back to visit your relative," he said in a loud voice.

He scanned his card to get them through the locked doors. "This better be good, and you better have cookies hidden on your person somewhere," he hissed under his breath when they were out of Brenda's earshot.

"No cookies *on me*, but I can get you cookies," Sadie assured him. "Any way I can get in to see Cody Carter?"

"Girl, no. They've got two officers out in front of his room and they're getting antsier by the minute. Your boyfriend was here a few hours ago when he first woke up and he looked like he'd caught himself a trophy trout when he came out of that room."

"Will's not my boyfriend," Sadie protested. Hector led her to a waiting area, and they both sat. He checked his watch. "I've got about five minutes before my patient in 107 demands another ice cream. What do you want to know from Cody Carter?"

"You'd ask him a question for me?"

Hector shrugged. "I'm bored," he whined. "They won't let us have our phones at the station anymore so I can't film or watch TikToks, and all my patients are nice, so I can't even be mean about them in my head. I could use some excitement."

"You're amazing, Hector."

"I know," he said. "You have three minutes to come up with your questions."

* * *

In the end, Sadie only needed two minutes.

Number one, and most importantly, what was he going to tell her the night before?

Number two, who hit him over the head?

Number three, did he know who Mike Smith was?

Once Hector had memorized the questions, he escorted her out of the hospital through a side door. "I'll text you," he told her. "I get an actual break in the next hour and I can get my phone out of my locker."

"I'll send cookies over this afternoon," Sadie promised. "And don't get yourself in trouble. It's not worth it."

"I won't," he promised, then disappeared back inside the door. Sadie was at the back of the hospital, so she had to walk all the way around the outside to get to her bike. While she was there, she took a minute to enjoy the view of the Tetons. The famed mountains weren't visible in most of town thanks to a butte that blocked the view, and Sadie always liked to get a glimpse of them when she could. After a minute, she started walking. She called Jorge, who was working the front counter at the bakery until he had to pick up his grandkids at three.

"*Jefa*," he answered.

"I know you're calling me boss and not saying heifer, Jorge, but every time it takes me a minute."

"Sign of respect, *jefa*," he reminded her. She really needed to get back to practicing her Spanish. The Duolingo owl had long ago given up on her.

"Right. Hey, can you get a box of cookies together and have them delivered to Hector at the hospital? He did me a favor and is requesting payment." She cleared her throat, thinking, then added, "*por favor, amigo?*" weakly.

"Sure thing, Sadie," Jorge said, laughing at her. "Hey, before you go. Ted Shultz was in here earlier asking for you."

Sadie stopped short. "Really? That's kind of weird." Ted wasn't a fan of Sadie's leftist agenda and never stepped foot in the bakery.

"He was agitated about something. I told him I didn't know where you were, but I'd keep an eye out."

"Great. Well, I've been meaning to talk to him anyway, so I guess I'll go looking for him next."

"Be careful, *mija*," Jorge warned her, his voice softening.

"*Gracias*, Jorge. I will."

Sadie hung up and started walking again, thinking. Why would Ted be looking for her? It had to do with Malcolm, right? She finally rounded the corner near the front of the hospital, then had to blink to make sure she was really seeing what she was seeing. Someone was depositing a brown box dripping with dark liquid into her bike basket. No. Not again!

"Hey!" Sadie yelled, running towards them without thinking twice. "Stop that!"

The figure, a tall person dressed in black, including a black hoodie pulled up over their head, glanced at her, then sprinted away.

"What the fuck?" Sadie shouted after them, running up to her bike to inspect it. The lock was still in place. The box was a little bigger than the one she'd received yesterday, but something red was leaking out of it again. Was this the other end of the horse? Why?

Shit. Now she'd have to interact with Will this morning, and that was not high on her list after the kiss they'd shared out of nowhere the night before and the lecture she'd gotten and the law he'd laid down that she'd immediately disregarded. But wait. Maybe she could catch the person who had left the packages! If it turned out they were the killer, maybe she could skip a lecture entirely.

Sadie hurriedly unlocked the bike and put on her helmet, then hopped on and pedaled in the direction the figure had taken off in. There, up ahead a block! Sadie could see them running down the sidewalk. She picked up the pace, pushing her legs as fast as she could. Her torn up, hungover, sleep-deprived stomach gave a lurch, but she ignored it. If she could push herself a little faster, she might catch them!

The person glanced back, and seeing her gaining on them, crossed the street in between traffic.

"Dang!" Sadie cursed. She was going to have to break some rules. She whizzed around a car waiting to turn, slipping in front of a truck that honked angrily at her. Sadie didn't blame them. She was being very irresponsible, but the person was even closer now. They were looking desperate. If they darted into a yard and started leaping fences, Sadie would be out of the chase. They ducked into an alley instead, and Sadie grinned. They were only a few blocks from her house, and she knew that alley. If she went the other way, she'd be able to duck through the deer path between the two middle lots and head the runner off midway through the alley. If she was fast enough.

She skidded around the corner and pumped her legs, hitting the bumpy dirt track at a much too fast speed but weathering it through sheer force of will and the benefit of her generous weight on the seat, then zoomed into the alley and screeched to a stop right as the runner reached her. Sadie finally got a good look at their face.

"Vivian Benson?" Sadie said, breath heaving, sweat pouring down her face. Her legs were screaming in pain from their hard use. Vivian bent over to breathe deeply, too. When Sadie had caught her breath, she got off her bike, peering at the box again. Tentatively, she lifted the lid, not taped this time. She sighed and looked at the pale-faced Vivian. "Girl, what the fuck?"

Chapter Sixteen

"Who gives a baker cupcakes?" Vivian wailed as she walked beside Sadie and her bike. "I felt so dumb as soon as I did it. And then you saw me!"

Sadie patted her arm. "I love cupcakes as much as the next girl." She examined the one she was munching on, angel food crumb with a strawberry filling and whipped frosting. "Did you make these?"

"No!" Vivian said, blushing. "That's the second-worst part of it. I bought them at the Hole Grocer! Who gives a baker a baked good from their competition?"

"They've really stepped their pastry game up," Sadie mused, shoving the rest of the cupcake in her mouth. "I noticed that this spring at the big town square yard sale. I might need to see if I can steal their baker for my new commercial bakery."

Vivian smiled weakly at her. They were approaching Teton Tots. Vivian had taken down the hood of her lightweight sun-protective running hoodie and her blonde ponytail was bouncing. They stopped in front of the building. Sadie could hear kids playing in the backyard and again wondered about what kind of man found the noise offensive. It sounded like pure joy to her.

"Now, why did you drop off cupcakes in my bike basket? How did you know it was my bike?"

Vivian gestured at a bench in their garden, and Sadie propped her bike against the fence before sitting with her. "I saw you park it from the main road while I was running back here from the elk refuge trail. I ran over here, grabbed the cupcakes, and put them in the basket. I never meant for you to see me."

"So, how was I supposed to know they were from you?"

"There's a card," Vivian said, head in her hands.

"Ah." Sadie must not have noticed it. "But again, why?"

"I spent yesterday working with my husband's social media coordinator for his store putting together a series of videos about Teton Tots and the value it brings to the community. It was your idea, and I wanted to thank you for it. We've already gotten tens of thousands of views and people are reaching out to the Radcliffes asking them to renew our lease!" Vivian pulled her phone out of her leggings pocket and pulled up a video, showing it to her.

Sadie grinned while she watched it. The kids were adorable, the production value was excellent, and the goals of the campaign were precise. "It's great, Vivian. If it doesn't convince the Radcliffes, I'm sure it will bring in a different opportunity for the center. I'll share it on the bakery socials, too." She handed her back her phone.

"Thank you," Vivian said. "Seriously."

"You bet. And while the cupcakes are great as a thank you, what I'd really like is for you to tell me what it is you're hiding about Malcolm."

Vivian's face fell. She swallowed hard, her eyes suddenly anywhere but Sadie's face. Then they locked in on the condos next door, specifically the one on the end across the tall fence where Malcolm had lived. She sniffled and wiped her eyes. "I didn't kill him," she said finally. "I didn't." She gulped. "At least, I didn't kill him on purpose."

Sadie's heart was pounding fast again. What did that mean? "Okay..."

"I was so mad. We serve this town's workforce. The billionaires don't send their kids to us. They have nannies if they have kids at all. It's the healthcare workers, the hospitality workers, the cops, the civil servants that send their kids to us. The people that work at the grocery store, the gas station, the laundromat. The people trying to make a living! And fucking Malcolm Radcliffe, who never had to work a day in his life, was going to shut us down because he could. I saw red."

"So you confronted him at his condo. You told me you didn't go inside."

"And I didn't! I did nothing to him. Directly."

Sadie got a weird feeling. "Did you...oh man, Vivian, did you poison his vape pen?"

"What? No! Can you even do that? That's...wait, is *that* what killed him?" She looked incandescent with relief then. "That's what did it? Then I really didn't kill him!"

"What did you do to him, Vivian?" Sadie's voice was hard.

"One of my husband's employees is a server at one of the boutique hotels and he mentioned that Malcolm had some allergies."

"Oh no."

"I didn't want to hurt him! And I don't think I did. I had nothing to do with his nasty vape pen. I just...sprinkled pepper on his door handle. And in his mailbox. And in the window of his car when it was open one time. And I might've mailed him an envelope full of it once when his lawyer sent a letter saying the kids shouldn't sing outside anymore."

"You could've killed him!" Sadie burst out. "He was deathly allergic to pepper."

Vivian was white as a sheet. "I didn't think it was like a death allergy. Just, you know, a little uncomfortableness. Maybe he'd have to stab himself with an Epi-Pen, which he definitely deserved. I wouldn't have done it if I thought it might kill him."

Sadie rubbed her eyes. She was getting a massive headache, and it wasn't just from her hangover. "When was this?"

"Oh, over the last few weeks. He's been hassling us nonstop. That last morning, though, was when I put pepper on his doorknobs. To his house...to his car. That might not have done anything to him, though, right? I'm sure he had to breathe it in or ingest it for it to affect him, right?"

"I guess...?" Sadie wasn't sure. Her cell phone buzzed in her pocket and she pulled it out. It was a text from Hector.

#1: MR isn't MR, #2: No idea, #3: MS is MR

Sadie frowned at the screen. Cody was going to tell her that Malcolm Radcliffe wasn't Malcolm Radcliffe, he didn't know who had hit him, and Mike Smith...was Malcolm Radcliffe. Her head was spinning.

"Vivian, did you ever see Ted Shultz over at Malcolm's house?"

Vivian thought about it. "No. But I saw them up at the Death Canyon trailhead a few weeks ago, probably the middle of July? I thought it was a little strange. I was headed for a run, and neither of them were dressed for hiking or running."

"So, they were having a meeting?"

"They were talking near their cars. It seemed a little tense, and when Malcolm saw me, he got in his car and left."

"What time of day was this?"

"It was early morning. My husband had the kids, and I was going for a ten-miler, so just before sunup."

"A weird time for a non-hiking meeting in the woods," Sadie

mused. While she considered that, her phone rang in her hand. Penny.

"Hello?"

"Police just released a statement saying that they found both the poison and tools to make the method of delivery in Cody's trailer, and have charged him with murder."

"Wait...but the poison was *horse medicine*. Common horse medicine, from what I remember! And Cody has a horse."

"Yeah, but sometimes a duck is a duck, Sadie," Penny said, snapping her gum. "I take it you didn't get to talk to him?"

"No, but I got a couple of answers out of him, anyway. Can you look into something for me? Cody says Malcolm Radcliffe wasn't really Malcolm Radcliffe, and was someone named Mike Smith, which was the name on the credit card Malcolm used. I can't figure it out."

"Hmmm...yeah, I'll look into it. And I'm going to get on Greg's case because that's something they would already know."

"I know," Sadie said. "They're keeping a lot close to their chests. But...I don't think it was Cody. My gut says it's not right, and I still don't get what his motivation would be. It seems like Malcolm was the one who had something to hide with the whole other name thing, not Cody." She'd lost Penny's attention, though. She was hissing something to Randall.

"Gotta go," Penny said. "Randall got a pencil stuck in his cast and he's allergic to graphite." She hung up.

Vivian was looking at her with suspicion. "Malcolm isn't Malcolm? But...we're petitioning Malcolm Radcliffe's dad to let us keep our building."

"I know," Sadie said. "It's incredibly confusing. Listen. You need to confess this to the police. I don't think you'll get in trouble, but if by any chance the pepper combined with the poison actually killed him...that might be the difference for a murder charge for Cody. Come clean."

Vivian sighed, brushing a tear from her cheek. "You're right. I would expect my kids to do the right thing. I need to do the right thing too."

Sadie patted her arm. "Text me when you tell them." She left the other part unsaid. Tell them, or Sadie would. She put her helmet on and mounted her bike again. "And thanks for the cupcakes," she called, biking away. After consideration, she turned left onto the main road. She needed to head north to the vape store. Ted Shultz could wait.

* * *

Heading north out of Jackson, Cache Street became the highway that led to Grand Teton National Park and eventually Yellowstone. The highway passed by the National Elk Refuge, which was right on the edge of town on the east side of the highway. On the west side was a Dairy Queen and a strip mall with a variety of shops in it. One of them was the vape store.

Sadie parked her bike outside and locked it. Last minute, she decided to bring the cupcakes.

The store smelled like cigars, tobacco, and something cloyingly sweet she couldn't identify. It was dim, with floor to ceiling displays and racks throughout the store, as well as a humidor in the back and a long, unoccupied counter with an impressive amount of stuff behind it. A bell on the door jingled as it shut behind Sadie, and a prim-looking white woman in a cardigan twinset and pearls came through the beaded curtain from the back room, smiling politely. Then she narrowed her eyes.

"You're Sadie Moose," the woman said. She was probably in her early fifties, and Sadie couldn't help but think she looked a little out of place in the store.

130

"Uh...I am. I'm sorry. Do I know you?" Sadie walked forward to the counter.

The woman sniffed. "I don't think so. I'm Tiffany Shultz."

Recognition bolted through Sadie. "Oh! Tiffany. Of course, I know you and Ted." *Her husband, Ted Shultz. Former friend of Malcolm Radcliffe. That had been looking for her earlier.* This might be harder than Sadie had thought it would be. She put the cupcakes down on the counter. "I just got these cupcakes and they're so good. Would you like one?"

Tiffany wrinkled her nose. "I don't eat sugar." With one finger, she pushed the box back towards Sadie.

"Okay," Sadie said, trying to sound upbeat. "Hey, I wanted to ask a question if I could?"

"Of course you do," the woman harrumphed.

Tough crowd. "Did Malcolm Radcliffe shop at this store?"

Her face flushed. "Our customers are strictly confidential."

"Okayyyy, I understand that. Hey, do you and Ted own this store? I didn't know that."

She put her shoulders back. "We do. This is one of several properties in the Shultz portfolio."

"Ah. Okay, that's great! Good for y'all. You know, I heard Ted was looking for me earlier. Is he around?"

Tiffany looked disgruntled. "I don't know anything about Ted looking for you. He should be at the t-shirt shop."

"Alright, well, I'm gonna go. Sorry to bother you. Thank you!" Sadie bolted through the door.

The Shultzes owned the vape store in town that Kaleb was pretty sure Malcolm shopped at. What a perfect opportunity to poison him! They'd once been friends and weren't anymore, but had been seen together just a couple of weeks ago at a clandestine location. Had Sadie stumbled onto something the police possibly didn't know? She thought of Cody, now handcuffed to his hospital bed, still gravely injured. Someone had done that to him. Had it been Ted? Tiffany? They'd both been at the rodeo. What lengths would they go to protect themselves?

Sadie got back on her bike and started peddling into town.

But why would the Shultzes hurt Cody?

What had Cody known about them?

Ugh. Maybe her theory wasn't that great after all.

But it was still before noon. She'd packed a lot into her morning. She could swing by Shultz's Shirts to talk to Ted, then she'd go home and take a nap.

Chapter Seventeen

Shultz's Shirts occupied the most visible corner on town square, at the corner of Cache and Broadway, right where the main highway turned to head towards the parks. It shared one wall with the Starbucks, Sadie's most annoying competitor in town because their fancy bathrooms and prime location drew tourists away from Moose's. Along the same block was a toy store, a boot and hattery, a photography studio that did old-timey portraits, and an ice cream shop. Sadie parked her bike at the town square and then fell in step with the droves of tourists crossing Broadway before stepping onto the wooden boardwalk and through the open door into the shop. A blast of cold air from the air conditioning hit her, cooling her sweaty skin. The temperature had dropped into the low nineties, starting its tumble for the year, but it was still too hot for Sadie. She couldn't wait for fall.

The shop was packed. Since it was a Friday in mid-August, she guessed she shouldn't be surprised. She didn't see Ted. A bored-looking teenager was working behind the counter. She decided to look around. Juliana had said she should check out what he was selling, that it gave their town a bad name. How bad could it be?

The front of the shop was full of normal stuff. Shirts with moose and bears and cowboys on bucking horses and the town name or the park emblazoned on them. There were hats and mugs and keychains and mouse pads and tote bags and ornaments and everything else you could imagine with similar logos. There was a section for local guidebooks and kids' books, including one of Sadie's favorites, *Who Pooped in the Park?* She decided she'd pick that one up for Luna. Never too early to normalize poop and start learning about animals.

It was towards the back of the shop, where it was a little dimmer, a little less browsed, that things got weird. There was a wall of pamphlets that touted various conspiracy theories, from 9/11 being an inside job to JFK being alive and a QAnon prophet to chemtrails to an entire section devoted to the 2020 election being stolen. Then there were the red hats, the "blue lives matter" flags, the confederate flags, and the political propaganda. It looked like the kind of stuff that was sold at roadside stands outside of right-wing rallies. Sadie could see why Juliana was uncomfortable with it. Sadie was uncomfortable with it. People could believe what they believed, of course, but was it right to promote conspiracy and hate in a cornerstone shop? How welcoming was this to tourists with diverse beliefs and values? What did it make them think about Jackson Hole and Teton County, which was a blue blip in a deep red state?

Of course, what room did Sadie have to talk? Her bakery publicly touted her values and beliefs from the stickers on the door to the causes they supported. Sadie shook her head. But no. Her bakery was welcome and inclusive of all. It didn't side with racism and authoritarianism. Sadie stepped out of the section and into a quiet corner to observe the shop. She saw more than one person see the back corner and promptly leave the building.

Maybe Ted would see a drop in business because of the merchandise, or...Sadie watched an enthusiastic group of college-age men find the corner and enthusiastically pick out a few flags. Or maybe he wouldn't. People had the choice of where to shop and who to support. For her, she'd buy the book for Luna elsewhere.

"What are you doing skulking around over here?" A gruff voice asked from behind her, and Sadie whirled around.

"Hey, Ted," she said, putting her shoulders back and meeting his eyes. "I heard you were looking for me."

* * *

"I was," he said. "Follow me."

Sadie hesitated for a minute, but the shop was full. If she screamed, someone would hear her. She followed Ted past the red hat corner and into a back room, and then into his grimy office. He gestured her inside, and Sadie went ahead of him reluctantly. He followed her, then sat behind his desk. At least he'd kept the door open.

"Sit," he demanded.

Sadie frowned, but she sat in the folding chair across from him.

"I heard you were asking questions about me and my relationship with Malcolm," he said, getting straight to the point.

How had he heard that? Sadie tried to think about who she'd asked. Had someone overheard her?

"I asked," Sadie said. "I didn't know y'all were friends, and it surprised me when someone said you were. Especially after what you said about him the day he died."

"Simple answer. We weren't friends."

"Okay..."

"We were acquaintances through the Playhouse board and saw each other socially because of that from time to time."

"I heard you fell out over the 2020 election. Not to...bring up a sore spot."

Ted's face darkened. "I know your politics, Sadie Moose. I'm not getting into it with you."

Sadie held up her hands. "Not asking you to. So you're saying you weren't friends with Malcolm. When was the last time you spoke with him before his death?"

"I can't remember."

"Huh. I heard you were seen with him in a remote location just a couple of weeks ago. What was that about?"

"Vivian Benson has a big mouth."

Sadie cringed inwardly. She should've put that more generally and kept Vivian out of it. "I didn't say I heard it from Vivian," Sadie hedged.

"It doesn't matter," Ted said. "That was a chance encounter. We exchanged pleasantries."

"A chance pre-dawn encounter at an isolated trailhead where neither of you appeared to be going for a hike."

Ted crossed his arms over his chest, mouth in a straight line.

"Who do you think killed Malcolm?" Sadie asked.

Ted thought about it for a minute. "Cody. That's what the police think, and I back the blue."

"Right. Right. Okay." Sadie sighed. "Do you know anyone by the name of Mike Smith?" She watched his face closely.

"No," Ted said, but Sadie had seen a flicker of something in his eyes. Recognition? Panic?

"Okay. You've been super helpful, Ted. By the way, I actually just saw Tiffany. I didn't know y'all owned the vape shop, too. What else do you own?"

"You sure are nosy."

"I've been told that before," Sadie conceded.

"A few residential buildings for lease," Ted said. "We have an eye to buy more if we can."

"Great," Sadie said. "It's great to keep that money local. Well, I guess I'll see you around." Sadie stood, headed for the door.

"Have a good day, Sadie. And Sadie?"

Sadie looked over her shoulder at him.

"Stay out of my business. Or else."

Sadie couldn't get out of the t-shirt shop quickly enough. Though she hadn't heard Ted leave his office behind her, she couldn't shake the feeling that he was still watching her, even as she caught her breath and got herself together on the boardwalk outside. Ted denied any culpability or relationship with Malcolm, but Sadie knew he'd lied to her. And he definitely knew something about Mike Smith. Sadie needed to figure it out, too. Maybe Penny had uncovered something. Someone jostled her on the boardwalk, and Sadie realized she couldn't use her cell phone where she was standing. She was impeding traffic. She walked down the boardwalk instead, then slipped into the toy store to look for the book she wanted to get for Luna.

She found an out of the way corner after saying hi to the woman behind the counter, then pulled out her phone to text Penny.

Any word on Mike Smith?

The three little dots popped up, letting Sadie know Penny was typing back.

*You mean the most common name in America?
Impossible to track down. Still looking. Greg
won't answer me.*

Be gentle with him.

Sadie sighed and put her phone back in her pocket. She'd need to do some research of her own. Maybe instead of looking for Mike Smith, she'd look for Malcolm Radcliffe. If Malcolm wasn't Malcolm like Cody insisted, then someone else was Malcolm. It should be easy enough to figure that out, at least.

Sadie headed for the book section, found the book she was looking for, got distracted by the adorable selection of stuffed animals, and ended up at the counter with the book and a stuffed moose, bear, and deer. She had zero restraint when it came to buying for her goddaughter.

Sadie chatted with the woman behind the counter while they finished the transaction, then took her bag to go. There was a set of low bins underneath the counter filled with small toys, perfect for young kids to beg for while their parents checked out. One bin was full of animals, including a very familiar-looking horse. Sadie paused, digging through the bin and pulling the horse out.

"That's been popular lately," the woman laughed. "The t-shirt shop guy even came by and bought one the other day. Said it was for his grandson."

Sadie studied the horse. It was the same one that had come to her, body-less, yesterday. "Wow," Sadie said. "Yeah, it's cute. A lot of people have bought it, though?"

The woman nodded. "Yeah, it was popular with a group of kids that came through with a youth group, too. I guess they'd all gone horseback riding as part of their camp and they wanted a souvenir."

"Oh, got it," Sadie said. "Cool." She put it back, heart racing. She waved bye to the woman, then walked out the door, straight to the ice cream shop a few doors away.

Ten minutes later, she sat on a bench in the town square, the toy store bag next to her and a cup of huckleberry ice cream in her lap. She was composing a text to Greg and Will, her first group text to both.

> *Ted Shultz bought the same horse that was sent to me at the toy store two days ago, according to the woman working there right now. And according to the teenager at the ice cream shop, his favorite ice cream is vanilla with extra strawberry syrup, which he gets almost every day, including yesterday. Ted was out looking for me today and when I found him, he told me to get out of his business or else. I think you should look closer at Ted for Malcolm's murder.*

There. That was concise. She hit the send button, then put her phone on silent and shoved it in her pocket. She didn't want to answer any of their questions. She raised a spoon of ice cream to her lips, savoring the creamy, sweet, but punchy berry flavor. It was the taste of summer. She watched the crowd in the square, enjoying a quiet moment in what had been a week of busy days.

"Sadie!" She turned towards the voice and waved at Amanda, who was walking towards her, a pile of papers in her hand. She held one out to her as she got closer, and Sadie took it. "We're having a memorial for Malcolm tonight," Amanda said, explaining the poster.

"Ah," Sadie said. "That's nice." She examined the poster. It had two pictures of Malcolm dressed for his various Playhouse roles and what she guessed was his professional headshot, and details about the memorial. Tonight at seven. At the Playhouse. Drinks and catering provided. "Wow," she said. "The Playhouse is giving up the Friday night show proceeds for this?"

Amanda shrugged. "I think Bob and Helen are trying to play nice, realizing that their attitude isn't helping them. The show was only half-full tonight anyway, so they offered refunds or credits. Sounds like most people just moved to tomorrow's show."

"Cool," Sadie said. "I'll be there."

She had some sleuthing to do.

Chapter Eighteen

A pounding at her door woke her several hours later. She stared at the clock by her bed groggily. 5:45. Morning or night? How long had she slept? Tyrone put his head on the side of the bed and nosed her, and Sadie realized it had to be night. Tyrone wouldn't have let her sleep through his normal dinner and evening outdoor play session. She'd slept a little less than three hours. It had done her good, though. Her stomach didn't have that dried out, hollow, hungover feeling, and her head no longer hurt. The pounding at the door came again and Tyrone barked, looking at her, then in the door's direction, then at her again.

Right.

She should get that.

She pulled on a pair of shorts from the floor to go with the tank top she'd slept in and stumbled in that direction. She peeked through the peephole. Her phone was buzzing in her hand, and she was grateful she'd replaced the battery in the video doorbell. She didn't need to check the camera feed, though. She recognized the angry face on the other side. Apparently, she was due for another lecture.

She opened the door and Will stormed past her.

"Hello to you, too," Sadie said, closing the door behind him and rubbing her eyes sleepily. He'd already barged into her kitchen, and she could hear him banging cabinet doors in search of something. Sadie wandered after him, Tyrone at her heels. "If you're looking for bourbon, it's in the cabinet above the freezer."

He opened the cabinet and pulled the bottle out, pouring a splash into the jam jar he'd found and tipping it back. He took a deep, calming breath then.

Sadie climbed into one of the chairs at the counter and patted the one next to her. "Come sit, big guy. Tell me what's going on. I hope I didn't make you this mad."

Will sank into the chair after filling the glass with water. He took another deep breath. "Vivian Benson just broke my entire case."

"Ah."

"Uh-huh."

"So...I suppose I kind of had something to do with this."

"You could say so."

"But...if her sprinkling pepper on doorknobs somehow contributed to Malcolm's death, then it's good it came out. It's all about the truth, right? That there were multiple factors in his death means something."

"So you're glad that nice woman might be charged with murder?"

Sadie gasped. "But that's not what killed him!"

"Exactly!" He burst out. "The poison killed him, but the pepper could've helped him along. It just makes things so complicated."

"So, did you have to let Cody go?"

"Yes, we dropped the charges. And I'm in deep shit with the DA's office for the whiplash."

Sadie was silent for a few minutes. "Well...is this a good

opportunity for you to listen to some of the things I know without yelling at me about how I know them?"

"I don't yell," he said, a muscle in his jaw ticking. "But I have been a little harsh. Purely out of worry for you. I apologize."

"Thank you. Now, are we ready to spill secrets to one another?"

Will checked his watch. "Nope. And you have about half an hour to get ready to go."

Sadie blinked. "I'm not up for a date tonight."

"Not a date. We're going to the memorial for Malcolm they're putting on at the Playhouse. Again, Sadie, when I take you on a date, you will know it's a date."

Right. Right. She'd set an alarm when she came home to nap earlier after the ice cream had heightened her lack of sleep and made biking around dangerous. "Right, I was planning on going. I guess we can go...together?"

"I don't want you in that room full of suspects without me," Will said. "You've already done enough damage." He tried to soften the blow with a wink.

Sadie gritted her teeth anyway. "And what about Ted Shultz sending me the horse head?"

Will blinked at her. "What?"

"I sent you and Greg a text!"

Will pulled his phone out of his pocket and scrolled through his texts. "I don't see it."

"Damn," Sadie said, stomping to her bedroom to get her phone. Cell service was often terrible in the center of town with all the tourists that calls were dropped and sometimes texts didn't go through. She pulled the text up and sighed, walking back into the room. "It didn't go through, and I didn't notice." She handed him her phone, and he read it.

"Huh."

"That's all you got? This was some A-plus sleuthing. And yet another threat aimed towards me. Which I know is a trigger for you."

"It's all circumstantial, but sure, we'll look into it. But why would Ted Shultz kill Malcolm? What's his motive?"

"I haven't gotten that far…but also, it's time for you to tell me about Mike Smith. I know you're hiding that whole thing."

Will shook his head. "Not sure how you found about Mike Smith, but we're keeping that close to our chests for now," he said. "Sorry."

"You and Greg suck," Sadie complained.

"Following the professional rules of my job definitely 'sucks'. Now go get ready. I'm going to take a nap on the couch while I wait."

"Okay, but only if you let Tyrone out." At that, Tyrone stood from where he'd sprawled on the anti-fatigue mat in front of the sink, tail wagging.

"You got it," Will said, heading for the backdoor. Sadie headed for the shower.

* * *

In the three days since Malcolm's death at the shootout, Sadie hadn't made it to the Playhouse yet, which in retrospect seemed like a gross oversight. She'd meant to go today, but what with being hungover, going on a bike chase, and being verbally abused by Tiffany Shultz and threatened by her husband, she hadn't really had the time.

As soon as they walked into the theater lobby, where everyone was gathering prior to the doors opening, Will stalked off. They'd talked about this on the way over. He had to do his very important detective-ing, and Sadie wasn't to distract him from it. She was on her own to do her thing, as long as she didn't leave his sight. Sadie had promised him she'd listen, but he hadn't seen her fingers crossed behind her back. Sadie took a minute to look over the crowd. Perhaps it was the free food and drink promised on the flyers distributed around town, but it was a much better turnout than she'd imagined it would be. In fact, there were plenty of people here that she not only didn't recognize, but who didn't seem to fit the Jackson Hole vibe. She smiled sadly to herself. Would Malcolm's memorial be largely attended by tourists?

Then she saw the crowd of Playhouse actors, including her dad, Robin on his arm as always, and she felt a little better. Amanda, Kaleb, Ed, and Jordan were there, too. Cody's absence was obvious and gave her a guilty pang.

She spotted a familiar swoop of pink hair and made her way through the crowd to Penny's side. She had her notebook out—this one was shaped like a cowboy boot—and was talking to Helen Foster. Sadie tuned into their conversation over the din of voices around them.

"—was an integral part of our company, and a beloved member of our board. We're very distressed over his passing and the possibility he was murdered."

"Possibility? Pretty sure the police are positive he was murdered."

Helen pressed her lips together unhappily. "I would like to believe no one in our community would do something so terrible."

"Hm," Penny said, looking through her notes. "You were out of town for the first shootout in two years?" She sounded skeptical.

Helen nodded. "I had a family emergency and had to fly back to Michigan. I didn't get in until the next morning. I'd planned my flight back in advance, of course."

"Have you spoken to any of Malcolm's family members?"

"Malcolm wasn't close with his family." She cleared her throat, pasting on a sorrowful expression. "We were his family, here at the Playhouse."

Sadie tamped down her sound of displeasure at the lie. She must not have done a very good job, because Helen's eyes flew to her. Penny nudged her, and Sadie coughed, hoping that might cover her foible.

Helen narrowed her eyes but looked back at Penny. "Now, if you'll excuse me, I need to open the doors to the theater. We are very grateful to everyone who came to honor Malcolm, and we hope they can contribute to his legacy." She turned and stalked away.

"His legacy?" Sadie asked.

"Oh yes." Penny flipped to a different page in her notebook. "The Malcolm Radcliffe Playhouse Modernization Fund, which she's announcing tonight."

"She's taking donations at his memorial?"

"She's ice cold. I love her," Kendall said from beside her. Claire waved from her side. The petite blonde was dressed for a much fancier theater, her white blonde hair swept up in a chignon.

The crowd started flowing into the theater, and the four of them let themselves be swept in, too. Kendall elbowed her way through to get them seats in the middle, fourth row back. "Save seats for Kamari, Max, Sage, and Gavin," she said, and they threw their bags and legs over the seats they needed.

Sadie looked around for Will but didn't see him. He was probably in the back, where he could see the entire theater. If Will was right, the killer wasn't there. He was still in a hospital bed across town. But even if Will was right, and it was Cody, who had bashed him on the head? Sadie thought it had been the real killer. Not Vivian. Sadie believed her pepper story. Maybe Helen or Bob? Helen was certainly taking advantage of

Malcolm's death. Or Ted Shultz? There was acrimony there, and he'd lied to her today, then threatened her. Plus, he owned the vape store Malcolm was rumored to shop at. Means, definitely. Opportunity, abundant. But what was the motive? And what was with the whole Mike Smith thing? Sadie really had to get to the bottom of that, but how?

The lights dimmed twice to signal the event was about to start, and people took their seats. Kamari, Max, Sage, and Gavin appeared and chose seats. Sadie exchanged greetings with them, then studied the stage. A large movie-size screen was set up on the stage, flanked by two massive, vibrant floral arrangements. A microphone stand and stool were the only other props. Sadie wondered what exactly they were in for.

She couldn't have predicted how the show would go.

Chapter Nineteen

s the lights dimmed, her phone buzzed in her pocket and she pulled it out. It was a text from a number she didn't recognize.

I told you to stay out of it. No more warnings.

Sadie swallowed hard, screenshotting the text and then blocking the number and deleting the text. She sent the screenshot to Will, then put her phone back in her pocket. She was in a theater surrounded by her friends, and she knew nothing the police didn't know at this point. Someone was trying to scare her, and she wouldn't let them. But as Helen walked out onto the stage to speak, she couldn't help but glance around the full theater. Was whoever had sent the text watching her?

Gavin, to her left, bumped her shoulder. "Okay, Moose?"

Sadie nodded. "Yeah, yeah, totally."

Helen spoke then. She welcomed them to the memorial and thanked them for coming. She introduced the program for the evening. First, they'd watch a video, then there would be an open microphone for anyone who wanted to talk about

Malcolm. They'd close out with one more video and a song, and then there would be food served next door in the dinner theater.

The stage lights dimmed, and the film began. Set to a somber instrumental, it showed pictures of Malcolm as a child Sadie could only guess had been ripped from the internet. Or, at least, Sadie guessed it was Malcolm? He didn't resemble the stocky, dark-haired man she'd known. But people changed a lot from kid to adult. The images quickly changed to the man she'd known. More images she'd imagined were taken from his social media accounts. Then his headshot, and photos from the productions he'd been in. Interspersed were videos of him on stage, as well as some behind-the-scenes content. There were laughs and some poignant moments, and Sadie saw a few people in the crowd getting emotional. It felt good that someone would miss him. She felt bad his family wasn't there.

The video ended with a still of him, faded to black in white, with In Memoriam and his years of life on the screen. The theater burst into applause.

After a few moments, Helen came back out.

"At this time, we'd like to welcome anyone up to the mic who'd like to say something about Malcolm, or perform a poem or song about him. We welcome artistic interpretations here," she tittered. "I'll begin. Malcolm and I didn't always see eye to eye—" there were snickers in the audience that quickly quieted down. That was an understatement, according to what Sadie knew. "But I respected him as a thespian, philanthropist—" a snort behind her that Sadie guessed belonged to Vivian Benson "—and lover of the arts. And he loved this place we call home, beautiful Jackson Hole. He was the adopted son of this valley. We here at the Jackson Hole Playhouse are proud that he was a part of our family, and we will continue his legacy for years to come."

Light applause. The community wasn't completely sold on

Helen's story. Helen stepped aside, and the mic was empty. There was a rushed silence, then whispers. Who would speak?

Sadie saw a few people stand, including her dad, and a queue formed stage left behind a tall, white, blonde-haired man Sadie didn't recognize. He was wearing an exquisitely tailored suit and walked with confidence to the microphone, then tapped it to make sure it was live. He squinted into the lights, took in the crowd.

"Well," he began in a crisp accent that spoke of posh education, "I don't know how to burst everyone's bubble, but that man in the video? That wasn't Malcolm Radcliffe." Murmurs spread throughout the crowd. Penny, to her right, gripped her arm tightly.

"Whattttt?" Kendall said loud enough only they could hear it. She was munching popcorn she must've brought from home.

"Plot twist," Max breathed.

"Drama," Sage agreed.

Sadie held her breath. The man was taking in their response. When they'd quieted again, he spoke.

"I'm Malcolm Radcliffe."

The theater erupted in gasps and excited exclamations. Sadie's and Penny's eyes met. "Mike Smith," they said in unison.

"Who?" Gavin said.

"I didn't think he looked like a Radcliffe," Claire mused. "The Radcliffes are all blonde. And tall. So tall."

"You could've said," Sadie said, aghast.

Claire examined her nails. "Not my business."

Helen rushed onto the stage to get the microphone from blonde-Malcolm, but he was holding it out of her reach, watching her attempts to grab it from him with amusement. Sadie saw Will at the other end of the stage, tense and ready to intervene if needed.

"Let him speak!" someone in the crowd behind them yelled.

"Yeah, let him speak!" Kendall shouted. Arlo repeated the call.

"Let him speak! Let him speak!" The crowd was chanting now. Penny was recording with her cell phone.

Helen finally gave up, stomping to the side of the stage to whisper angrily at Will. Blonde-Malcolm motioned for everyone to quiet so he could speak.

"My name is Malcolm Radcliffe. My father is Milton Radcliffe, an investor you may have heard of. I grew up in Gilroy, California. When I was at Stanford freshman year, I roomed with a kid named Mike Smith. Mike was a scholarship kid from Nevada. He was nice. We were both into acting. He dropped out mid-year because of a family emergency and I never spoke to him again. This was over twenty years ago."

He paused again, and Sadie could tell blonde-Malcolm had a flare for the dramatic.

"The man you're all here to mourn is that man. Mike Smith."

Again, the room erupted into shouts and excited chatter. Will walked onto the stage, motioning for blonde-Malcolm to put the mic away and step away with him. Helen grabbed the microphone as soon as it was back in its holder.

"This is just one man with a story. We don't know it's true," Helen screeched. "Respect Malcolm, who we're here to mourn."

With timing so perfect Sadie guessed a disgruntled audiovisual tech was behind it, the screen behind her flicked back on, showing a screen asking for donations to The Malcolm Radcliffe Playhouse Modernization Fund. Included was a QR code, Venmo code, PayPal code, and where donations could be directed at the local bank.

"You're only doing this to make money!" someone yelled, and the crowd agreed, roaring along.

"We're honoring his memory by taking donations to improve the theater he loved!" She shouted, and the mic squealed, then cut out. Apparently, the AV tech was done with her. Sadie felt conflicted. Malcolm had loved the theater. But Helen had been a little on the nose with the donations. It hadn't even been a week.

Arlo stepped onto the stage then, talking into Helen's ear and then taking the mic away. Helen, visibly upset, shuffled off the stage. Sadie saw Bob wrap her in his arms offstage, and she sighed. At least they had each other.

Arlo tapped the mic meaningfully, eyebrows raised at the AV box, and the mic turned back on.

"Well, this has been dramatic," Arlo said, and the riled-up crowd laughed. "I'm not sure we've had this much drama here since a live round made it into a prop gun during Annie Get Your Gun in eighty-seven, actually," he mused, and there were more laughs.

"Only funny because no one was hurt," Sadie muttered, and Gavin muffled a laugh next to her.

"So, there's some question as to who exactly we're all here for." The crowd quieted. "But I don't need to know the exact name of the man to mourn him. I worked alongside him, and we shared laughs and good times. I don't know that I'd call him a great actor—" more laughs "—but he loved the stage." Applause, first small, then raucous. Arlo nodded at the crowd, waving his hand for them to be quiet.

"Now, I think we could all use a drink. Let's go."

The crowd clapped and stood, shuffling out of the theater to exit into the dinner theater, a smaller restaurant-style space they used for family friendly dinner entertainment seasonally. Sadie wasn't sure how everyone was going to fit and hoped Helen had made enough food for everyone. That crowd would riot if it was a cash bar.

"Well," Kendall said, tipping her bag of popcorn into her mouth to capture the last of it, "that was the most exciting thing I've ever seen here."

Penny stood and started squeezing past everyone's knees. "If I don't talk to the new Malcolm, Randall will kill me," she explained.

"Good luck," Sadie said. "I doubt he's still in the building." But she was talking to her back as she rushed the stage.

"Should we go get a drink?" Kamari asked.

Kendall shook her head. "I don't feel like fighting through there."

"Let's go to my place," Gavin suggested. "I have a new recipe and cocktail I want to try, and I stocked the fridge with some brews to test."

"Uh, best offer I've had in days," Max said. Sage nodded agreement.

"Alright," Sadie said. "Let's go."

Briefly, as she left the theater with her friends, she remembered her promise to Will to stay within his sight, but he'd abandoned her with blonde-Malcolm. What kind of danger could she be in, surrounded by this group? Kendall was a black belt, Claire had bodyguards that were certainly lurking somewhere, Kamari was an elite athlete with amazing strength and speed, Max was so tall they could see anyone coming and had baker's arms, Sage could deescalate any situation, and Gavin probably had a knife on him somewhere. Not for fighting, but to cut a nice salami if he came across one.

And Sadie?

Well, she could scream. And she had a phone. And she loved her friends more than anything on earth, so she wasn't about to allow anything bad to happen to them because of what she was involved in.

Chapter Twenty

While Gavin worked efficiently on the new recipe he wanted them to try, everyone else sat at a table pushed over to the side in the kitchen, sipping beers and talking over what had just happened. Baxter and Sully, Claire's two bodyguards that she called her driver and assistant, had joined them. Kendall was recounting the story of what had happened. Apparently they'd been in the car the whole time and had missed the show.

"So then the dude is all, 'I'm Malcolm Radcliffe'!"

"No!" Baxter, the driver, exclaimed. He was a mountain of a man from Hawaii with thick black curls and a boisterous laugh. He had been a tackle in the NFL for years before retiring because of a knee injury.

"I didn't think he looked like a Radcliffe," Sully, the assistant, said, and Claire nodded vigorously at him. Sully was a tall, thin, white man with a nasally voice and a tendency to always have some sort of face injury. Today it was a butterfly bandage over a busted eyebrow that he'd declined to explain.

Kendall recounted the rest of the story. "And then Helen

tries to get the mic—" Sadie's phone rang, and she glanced down at the screen. Will.

"Gonna take this," she whispered, slipping out of the kitchen and into the darkened dining room. It was weird to see the normally bustling restaurant dark, tables pushed to one side, chairs stacked, the room half renovated and half still the classic Italian restaurant she'd grown up going to for celebratory dinners. She slid into the booth that she'd sat in for her high school graduation dinner, answering the call.

"Sadie." Will sounded worried. "Where did you go?"

"I'm with Gavin and friends at his restaurant," Sadie said. "I thought you left with blonde-Malcolm, so..."

"Blonde Malcolm?" Will sounded amused. "Well, you can call him just Malcolm. The secret's out. The Malcolm Radcliffe who died in that stagecoach was actually Mike Smith. He'd been using Malcolm's identity for years to gain clout and explain his money."

"So he did have money?"

"He had some, at least when he came here, but he wasn't rolling in it. One of my guys got a hit on a lottery win in California the same year he supposedly left Stanford for a family emergency. We're thinking that's the money he's been throwing around."

"But the stagecoach renovation...the lighting system, all the money he's poured into that theater, that's a lot of money. Plus the condo, the clothes, the lifestyle..."

"Debt, for one, and we think he might've been getting money through...less than legal means."

"So he really was a scammer?"

"You thought he was?"

"It was a theory that was floated," Sadie admitted. "How did he get away with saying he was that Malcolm Radcliffe though? He was on social media, websites?"

"Malcolm has lived overseas for years. He flew back in when his father contacted him to make sure he was alive and hadn't died in Jackson Hole. He came out here to see who had been using his name."

"And decided the best way to out him was at his memorial? That's cold."

"It seemed efficient to him. Plus, he liked the drama of it."

"Huh. So what does this all mean for the case, then? Who the hell killed Malcolm...I mean Mike Smith?"

"No comment," Will sighed. "And I don't know who's threatening you, either. But, I've got my hands full. Jaden's mom's going to meet me in Idaho Falls tomorrow. He's going home a little early because of all this."

"Oh, Will, I'm sorry. What a bummer end of the summer for him."

"Yes, and no. Bummer for me, but his babysitter is his favorite person on earth, so he had a good enough time. I'll be out of town from the morning until around noon. Promise me you'll stick close to your friends? I'll send a patrol by your house a few times overnight. Call Greg immediately if something happens."

"Okay," Sadie said. "I can do that. But before you go—this new information—does it clear my dad?"

There was silence for a few minutes. "I can't clear anyone, but I don't think your dad did it, Sadie."

"Thanks, Will. Drive safe, tell Jaden bye from me."

"I will," he promised, and hung up.

Sadie sat for a minute, taking in the information he'd told her. A scammer. Malcolm—Mike—had been a scammer.

Had that gotten him killed?

* * *

Over dinner served family style in the kitchen, Sadie told her friends the news. When she'd finished, she served herself a generous portion of cucumber fennel salad to start.

"So whoever killed him was probably someone he scammed," Kamari said.

"That make sense," Sadie agreed. "I feel like this opens the entire case back up. Malcolm's—listen, I'm just going to keep calling him that, okay? I can't stop." The table agreed. "His world seemed small to me. The Playhouse, that was basically it. But he could've been scamming anyone. Someone not local, even. Without access to all his electronics and stuff, I don't know how I could solve this one."

"So we have to leave it to the cops?" Baxter said, frowning. He didn't make a habit of getting involved with cops and had a general disregard for their abilities.

Sadie shrugged. "I guess so." She felt lousy about it. On the one hand, Arlo was mostly out of the picture as a suspect. She'd done enough for him, which had been her true goal. But on the other, she felt bad for Cody, who was still in the hospital with a recovery ahead of him and suspicion still clouding his reputation. And she felt for Vivian, who had made some poor decisions that Sadie had a hard time blaming her for. And she even felt bad for Helen, who truly loved the Playhouse and wanted the best for it. She might've been clunky about asking for donations, but her heart had been in the right place. Malcolm had loved the theater. What a legacy for him. Sadie wondered if the donation fund would be named The Mike Smith Playhouse Modernization Fund instead. Most likely, it would cease to exist completely.

Really, the only person in this scenario she didn't feel bad for was Ted Shultz. Because he was an asshole.

Gavin squeezed her shoulder, then plated a portion of wood-fired salmon onto her plate, garnishing it with the puttanesca sauce she had chosen earlier in the week and adding crisp potato wedges tossed in lemon zest and parmesan too. "Eat up," he told her. "Food solves everything."

And it did. Together with some of her favorite people in the world, talking about anything and everything that wasn't the case that had stumped her, eating Gavin's delicious food and talking about his life's dream coming true, taste testing several signature cocktails, laughing a lot and smiling so hard her cheeks hurt, her soul warmed. With her friends around her, she was safe, and she was fine, just as she was. It was okay if she wasn't the best amateur sleuth in the world. It was okay if she partied too hard once a year and got a hangover. It was okay if she couldn't quite figure out her love life. Her friends loved her the way she was, and she loved them, too.

Sadie climbed into bed at a reasonable hour that night. Kendall was again sleeping on the couch despite complaining about how stiff the new ones were. Claire had offered Baxter and Sully, but Sadie had declined. The last threatening text had told her to stay out of it. And now she was out of it. Surely it would be over now. She fell asleep to white noise, Tyrone snoozing in the bed at her feet.

Chapter Twenty-One

The first customer in the door when Moose's opened at seven was blonde-Malcolm. Sadie stared at him, slack-jawed, from the counter, while Rachael greeted him and took his order.

"A black coffee," Rachael said, jabbing her when she continued to just stare at him, even after he'd moved to the pickup section after paying.

"Right," Sadie said, jumping into motion. She had so many questions for blonde-Malcolm, but she hadn't had near enough coffee to ask them. She poured his to-go cup of coffee, then paused before handing it to him, taking a minute to peer at the cup like it had a name written on it.

"Um, black coffee for the real Malcolm Radcliffe?" she called out while winking at him.

Blonde-Malcolm laughed. "I take it you were at the theater last night," he said charmingly. "You should see the looks I've been getting all morning."

"And it's early," Sadie joked. "I imagine it will only get worse by noon."

"I'll be out of here by then," blonde-Malcolm said. Rachael

handed over a to-go container with a fork sticking out of it. He must've ordered a slice of quiche.

"You're headed out already?"

"I am. I gave my statement to the police. I caused a ruckus last night, and now I'm heading back overseas. My father's lawyers can do the rest."

So he really was a billionaire playboy.

"My work is piling up," he clarified when he saw the look on her face. "I run a micro-loan program for entrepreneurs in the developing world."

"Oh," Sadie said. "That sounds like rewarding work."

"It is," he said, flashing a bright white smile. "You can tell anyone who comes in here to talk about me I'm not so bad now, right?"

"I'll do my best," Sadie said wryly.

"Thanks. I'll give your bakery a five-star review in exchange." And then he waved and was out the door.

* * *

Sadie was rolling out scone dough later that morning when she thought of it.

Who had purchased Teton Tots, then?

If Mike-Malcolm didn't have any money left and was late on his rent, who had bought it? Vivian had confronted him with the lease termination, but he'd said all communication needed to go through his lawyers. Who were his lawyers? Sadie had presumed it was some out-of-town law firm that served his dad, but Mike-Malcolm didn't have fancy out-of-town lawyers. Who had served all the notices?

She cut the scones, placing them on the baking trays to bake, and cleaned up after herself. Her prep was minimal for the day, and it was relatively slow. Sage was handling everything in the back, and Rachael was in the front.

"I'm going to go into my office for a bit," she told Sage, pulling off her dirty apron and putting it in the soiled bin. She grabbed a cooked scone off a rolling rack and pushed into her office.

The county clerk's website was clunky, but she could access property records. The deed of sale had gone through last month. The new owners were...TTSH LLC.

The same owners of the new building next to Carloni's.

Where else had she heard that before? She navigated to the county GIS map, zooming in on Teton Tots on the satellite view. She clicked it. TTSH LLC was listed as the most recent owner. She clicked on the condo next door, Mike-Malcolm's condo.

TTSH LLC.

So he *had* bought it? And was also behind the new building? How?

She scrolled around the map, clicking on random buildings while she thought. She scrolled to the bakery, reading the name of the investment company that owned her block. Same as it'd been for close to a decade, and hopefully it would stay that way for a while. The current owners were committed to keeping the established businesses on the block. Sadie was sure she'd have to fight the battle to keep the block from being demolished and replaced by some luxury monstrosity again eventually, but she hoped it wouldn't be soon.

She kept clicking around on the map, this time around the town square. It was interesting to see what had changed. When Sadie was growing up, most of the buildings had been owned locally, but a lot of them were now owned by out-of-state conglomerates that leased to businesses, some local, some not, but they all gave off the air of being local. She clicked the ice cream store. The boot and hattery. The toy store. Starbucks. Schultz's Shirts. The jewelry store on the other side of the street.

And then she gasped, eyes widening. She clicked back on Shultz's Shirts. It was owned by TTSH LLC.

TTSH.

Ted.

Tiffany.

SHultz.

TTSH.

"*Holy shit.*" Sadie sat back, letting that sink in. Then she sat forward, zooming over to the vape store. The entire mini mall was owned by TTSH LLC.

This is one of several properties in the Shultz portfolio, Tiffany had said.

Several properties. A new office building by Carloni's. The mini mall. The corner building that housed Shultz's Shirts. Mike-Malcolm's condo. And now Teton Tots.

So it hadn't been Mike-Malcolm kicking the kids out of the center. It had been the Shutlzes. They'd let him take the fall. Why had he gone along with it?

Because they knew his secret. That had to be it. The Shultzes had found out Mike-Malcolm's secret, maybe when his rent fell behind, and they'd used him as a fall man for them to make a hugely unpopular move. They probably wanted to demolish Teton Tots and replace it with more condos like Mike-Malcolm had lived in. Or had it gone back even further? Had all Mike-Malcolm's complaints about Teton Tots been pushed by the Shultzes?

Who had the scammer really been? Was it Mike-Malcolm, using someone else's identity for clout but still using the credit card in his real name? Or had it been the Shultzes, manipulating someone to keep their own names clean?

Sadie needed to tell someone. She needed to tell Will! She glanced at her watch. But he would still be on the road to Idaho Falls with Jaden. He was probably out of cell service while driving through the mountains to Idaho Falls. So not Will. Greg! He'd said call Greg.

Sadie pulled out her phone and dialed Greg, hands shaking. She'd figured it out! The missing piece! She wasn't surprised the cops hadn't figured this out. It was subtle. It was much less in-your-face than a pile of ivermectin in Cody's trailer or Vivian sprinkling pepper on doorknobs.

The phone rang and rang, and he didn't answer. *Dangit.* "Greg, call me," she said, leaving a voicemail. She sent him a text, too, then tried Penny. No answer.

"Ugh." She drummed her fingers on her desk. How was she supposed to sit on this until someone got back to her? Fuck it, she was going to the police station. It was only a few blocks away, and it was broad daylight. She pushed her phone back into her pocket and hurried out of the office.

She was stepping into the alley behind the bakery when she realized she hadn't told anyone where she was going. That was dumb. She stuck her head back inside. "Sage! I'm going to the police station. Should be back soon."

Sage nodded her head in acknowledgment, peering into the mixer.

Perfect. She was going to get this information where it needed to be immediately.

* * *

Sadie could walk a couple of different routes to get to the police station, but something told her she should take the route that would take her by Mike-Malcolm's condo. It had been the key to the whole thing. She made a mental note to always use the map functionality when looking up property records from then on. If she'd done that before instead of just using the lookup function, she probably would've checked Teton Tots and seen the information days ago, before Cody was injured, before everything had happened with blonde-Malcolm. They might've already locked up Ted. Or Tiffany. Or both.

She was passing in front of Mike-Malcolm's condo, noting how quiet Teton Tots was on a Saturday, when she saw something out of the corner of her eye. She thought it might be a bluebird, but when she turned her head to look, she saw it was a blue shirt. A blue shirt on Ted Shultz's back, where he was carrying a bag of garbage out of Mike-Malcolm's condo and putting it into the bed of his truck. *Shit*. Had the police cleared the crime scene already, and now the building's owners were cleaning out his things? But the building owners were the *bad guys*! They could throw away evidence! Sadie ducked behind a bush between Teton Tots and Mike-Malcolm's building, hiding behind it. She needed to do something.

At a loss, she pulled her phone out of her pocket. She could at least take a couple of pictures. Yes! She'd take a couple pictures, then text them to Greg along with a 911 call me message. That would work. She raised the phone, snapping a few pictures of Ted taking out another load. There. That would do it. She opened her text message string with Greg, attaching the pictures and typing the message.

Then she felt the cool edge of a knife blade against her neck.

Chapter Twenty-Two

"Drop your phone," Tiffany Shultz said. "Drop it or I kill you right here."

Sadie dropped her phone. Both from the hard promise in Tiffany's words and from the numb tingling of adrenaline pumping through her veins. She couldn't feel her fingers anymore. Her heart pounded. She was afraid to swallow, to breathe. She felt a rising tide of panic. She knew it well, fought hard to keep it from confusing her when her brain and body were lying to her about there being something to panic about. But now. Now there was a reason to panic.

"Slowly walk forward. Try to run, and I'll cut you." Tiffany was short, but so was Sadie, so it was easy for Tiffany to walk behind her, one arm around Sadie's neck with the blade pressed against her pulse point. She held Sadie's arms behind her back as they shuffled forward into the space between the fence and the building that led back to the alley.

When they reached the alley opening, Ted was coming out of the back of the condo with more white garbage bags. He snarled when he saw her.

"I told you, Sadie Moose. No more warnings. Get her inside."

Things were a little blurry for Sadie after that. They pushed her inside the condo. She saw the house had been torn apart with papers everywhere. They were looking for something. Then they shoved her inside a spacious coat closet and shut the door. Sadie laid on the floor of the closet for long minutes, her body tense, listening to the surrounding environment.

Her heart was still pounding. Her tongue felt swollen and prickly in her mouth as panic threatened to take over. She realized she was breathing shallowly and erratically.

Well.

That wouldn't do.

She grasped for any strategy to get through without passing out. Or maybe passing out would be better. Maybe she'd sleep through whatever truly awful thing they were going to do to her.

She put a hand over her mouth to muffle the scream she felt building up.

Pull yourself together, Sadie Moose, she told herself sternly. Think about Tyrone. You're the only one who knows his favorite way to be petted. She pictured Tyrone's big, brown eyes in her head. She remembered how soft his ears were. She thought about how he sometimes smelled like Fritos and that meant he needed a bath, but how it was also a good smell. She thought about his happy bark, the one he made when he saw someone he liked. Her breath slowed. Okay. That was working.

She opened her eyes. She was on her back. The closet was walk-in size, not a normal coat nook. It was dark, but her eyes were adjusting. There was a row of coats and shoes along one wall, a row of shelves along the other. It smelled like leather and GORE-TEX. Her eyes focused on the ceiling. There was a light up there. Was there a light switch inside? They hadn't bound her or put anything over her mouth. She was free to move around. This had been impromptu, after all. They hadn't expected to run into her. Was there something in this closet she could use as a weapon?

She slowly made herself move her body, bringing feeling back into the limbs heavy from the exhaustion of panic, getting up onto her knees, then her feet, and exploring the space. Some of the shoes were heavy leather with pointed toes. That might hurt if she could fling one at someone. She worked her way towards the back of the closet, then around to the shelves.

By the time she was back to where she'd begun, she had a plan.

Working quickly but quietly, she piled most of the coats into a corner. She pulled the pointiest shoes into the pile, along with the bottle of bleach she'd found on a shelf of cleaning supplies. The shoes would make excellent bleach bombs. Then she unzipped the ski bag in the back corner, unclipping the skis from one another and putting them within her reach. She climbed into her fort. Hopefully, when they opened the door, they'd have to come close to her and she could throw the bleach bomb shoes at them, then knock them over the head with the skis. Now that she was set, she settled in to listen.

She'd lost track of how long she'd been there. She hadn't heard any noises since she'd come out of her panic, and anything that had been said through the door or any noises that had been made were a mystery to her. She sat, poised, for so long her butt started to hurt. The bleach smell was starting to make her head spin. Maybe she should've held off pouring it into the shoes. Then she started wondering if she was truly locked in. Had they thrown her in and then fled? She hadn't tried the door. Would a normal closet lock from the outside? But they could've used a chair under it or something. She should try it, or at least listen at it. But what if she got close to the door, and then they opened it and she was without her weapons?

How long had it been? Sage knew where she was. Would Sage sound the alarm when she hadn't returned shortly like she'd said? She thought back to that interaction. Sage had nodded, right? She had.

But she'd also had on big, over-the-ear headphones. Shit.

Had she really heard her, or had the nod Sadie thought she'd seen been her bopping along to a beat? It was possible no one knew she'd been headed to the police station then. The calm she'd felt when she'd come up with the plan started to fade, and she felt panic again. Now that she thought about it, the closet was a little small. She didn't like small spaces.

No! She would not panic again. She had a plan. If her legs started to go numb, she'd stand. She needed to be able to move swiftly when the door opened. And she had left a message for Greg telling him to call her. He knew she had some sort of information. Maybe he'd go looking for her, and when he found out no one knew where she was, he'd start searching. If nothing else, she'd planned to canvass with Paige that afternoon, so if she didn't show up by then they'd know something was up. She wished she had her phone. It was probably in a trash bin by now. It was clearly past time for her to invest in a smartwatch. Maybe she should put one of those tracking buttons into her shoes or something so someone could always find her. For next time.

Because there had to be a next time. This wasn't the end for Sadie. It couldn't be the end.

* * *

She was in the same position long enough she did eventually stand to stretch her legs. Her eyes had adjusted so well to the darkness she did another lap around the closet to see if she could find anything else. A gun? Was that too much to ask? But none of the boxes on the shelves and none of the pockets of the coats held a knife, a machete, a derringer, or even a prop gun. She was getting settled back into her coat fort when she heard voices outside the closet.

She crouched, pulling one of the coats over her head. It was all about the element of surprise, right?

She listened as hard as she could through the tweed covering her. Sweat dripped down her face. She struggled to control her breathing.

The voices were muffled, and she couldn't understand them, but they were getting closer.

With no warning, the door was flung open. Sadie stayed put.

"Get up!" Ted yelled from the doorway. She didn't move. "Get up!" He yelled again.

"Did you do something to her?" Tiffany shrieked from beside him.

"What would it matter?" Ted grumbled. "We're going to kill her, anyway. So does it matter if she's hurt now?"

"I don't want to clean this room," Tiffany whined.

"Shut up," Ted said. "Get up!" He shouted again into the room. He stepped closer. Sadie held her breath.

Another step.

Another.

Tiffany was right behind him. She could see their dark forms against the light through the weave of the fabric. *Hold tight, Sadie,* she told herself. Let him get one more half step closer...

Ted took the half step, and she burst into action, pulling off the coat with her left hand and throwing a bleach shoe in Ted's face with the right. It was a direct hit thanks to the close quarters. He screeched, wheeling back, almost taking Tiffany with him, but Sadie threw two shoes her way, too, before grabbing the ski propped on the wall beside her.

"You bitch!" Ted yelled, scrubbing at his eyes while Tiffany wailed.

"This is cashmere!" She screamed, plucking at her wet sweater, her eyes streaming.

They were both so distracted and half-blind they didn't notice her jabbing Ted in the stomach with the ski, and he toppled over. Then she whacked Tiffany's legs out from underneath her. She leapt over their prone forms, ski still in hand. She was two feet from the closet door. From there, it was a left, and then she could run out of the condo and into the alley, screaming for help. She was so close.

A meaty hand gripped her ankle, and she stumbled, screaming.

She looked down at Ted's red, twisted face. He would not win. She brought the ski down on his wrist with all the force of her baker's arms and there was a loud, sickening, crunching sound. He let go, screaming. She burst out of the closet, struggled at the backdoor for a half-second before opening it, and burst out into the alley, screaming.

Right into Greg. Behind him was what looked to be the entire Jackson Hole Police Department. Greg gripped her arms, holding her up as her legs buckled underneath her.

"Get on the ground, Ted, get on the ground!" Someone behind her yelled, and then everything was a blur. She was shuffled away from the scene while the police yelled at the Shultzes.

Greg helped her towards a cop car at the end of the alley, and when Sadie drew near, Kendall flew out of the passenger side door, tears streaming down her face. She wrapped her up in her arms and held her while Sadie broke down, sobbing. The yelling behind them continued, but for her, it was over.

Chapter Twenty-Three

"It actually set the record for the longest standoff in Jackson PD history," Will said. He folded the restaurant menu and put it down in front of him. "Is this really what you want to talk about?"

Sadie sat across from him, her own menu untouched. It had been one week since the Shutlzes abducted her, held her hostage in Mike-Malcolm's closet, then barricaded themselves inside for over seventy-two hours before surrendering into custody. During the standoff, they'd posted their manifestos in increasingly unhinged YouTube videos. Their final one had declared Sadie to be a lizard person possibly in charge of the New World Order.

It was an enormous responsibility to shoulder, being a lizard person in charge of a shadowy international underground government, so Sadie had taken the week off work, Robin and Arlo filling in for her. She'd spent her time relaxing, sleeping, reading smutty books, eating chocolate, trying to feel her feelings about the encounter so they wouldn't sneak up on her later, and of course, going over the mystery obsessively in her mind.

How had she figured out the missing piece, and the police hadn't?

"How about we set a time limit?" Sadie said. "Let's order, and we can talk about it through the appetizer, and then once our mains come, we stop. And that's it."

"Deal," Will said. "So it's police business until our main courses, then this is a date."

"Yes," Sadie agreed. "It's the date that I owe you because of your help last spring."

"Oooh, but now I owe you a date for solving my case for me and being kidnapped in the process."

"Already asking for a second date. How forward of you." Sadie opened her menu to hide her smile. In the week since Will had driven back from Idaho Falls at truly unsafe speeds, once he'd heard what had happened, he'd been apologetic and gracious with her. Even gentle. He'd even mostly held off on lecturing her.

"Ready to order?" The suave waiter appeared next to them, topping off their waters. They were at Elk & Olive, a long-running fine dining restaurant a few blocks off the Main Street. Sadie's parents had gotten engaged there a lifetime ago.

They both put in their orders—stuffed mushrooms and bread to share, elk tenderloin for Will and huckleberry scallops for Sadie, plus a bottle of pinot noir—and then Will took a drink of water, clearing his throat.

"Everything I'm about to tell you must stay between us, of course. And it will have to be proven in a court of law if the Shultzes don't take a plea, which frankly they'd be stupid not to, considering they basically admitted to everything publicly online, but that's not for me to say."

"Of course," Sadie said.

The wine came, and they did the tasting rigamarole, and then Sadie settled in with her glass to hear the complete story.

"Well. Ted and Mike were pretty close friends when Mike first moved here. They met at the Playhouse when Mike brought the money to redo the sound system and he presented the plan to the board from the perspective of a community citizen. After that, he just got closer and closer to both the Playhouse and the board. He kept bringing money, but only contingent on him being able to audition for certain roles, but it was obvious if he didn't get what he wanted, the money wouldn't keep coming in. The board went along with it because they weren't getting the money from anywhere else. Especially during the pandemic years. Things were tough when they were closed. Eventually, Mike got his seat on the board. He moved into that condo the Shultzes own in 2019. But then Mike and Ted had a falling out over the 2020 election."

"Mmmhmm," Sadie said. She knew all of this.

"Well, after their falling out, Ted found out that Mike wasn't who he said he was."

"How?" Sadie asked. That was still unclear to her.

"Looking at it from our perspective now, how didn't he find out? The Radcliffes are private people, but there are publicly available pictures of them as a family, and Mike is not in any of them."

"Huh."

"Anyway, Ted and Tiffany saw that as an opportunity. Mike already had a reputation as someone who liked to throw money around and someone who was self-absorbed, so they confronted him and blackmailed him into starting his war with Teton Tots in hopes the center would move out on their own."

"And when that didn't work, they bought it, but made it look like Mike had done it."

"Yep."

Their starters came, and they were quiet for a minute while they buttered bread. "It was that important to Mike, that he be known as Malcolm, that he followed through with that? I wonder why."

"We'll never know." Will shrugged. He popped a mushroom in his mouth, then opened it wide, blowing around it and making a pained, breathy noise before choking it down. "Jeez," he said, taking a gulp of water.

Sadie suppressed a laugh. "I do the same thing every time. I should've warned you. They're hot."

"I'm not going to be able to taste anything else all night," he whined.

"We're on a timer here, my dude," Sadie reminded him.

"Right. So then Cody joined the shootout act this year, and it turned out Cody knew Mike wasn't Malcolm because he'd gone to school with the real Malcolm's little sister. Cody and Mike started hanging out, and it made Ted nervous because he thought Mike was going to come clean to the community with Cody's support, and that's when they decided to kill Mike. Ted had a pile of ivermectin saved up from the pandemic when he'd stockpiled it, the bastard, and after researching it, he started grinding it up and adding it to the vape refills that Mike bought. Tiffany made sure the bad bottles made it to him and him alone. It took about two weeks for it to kill him."

"And the pepper had nothing to do with it?"

Will took a more cautious bite of a mushroom, nodding. "As far as the coroner can tell, yes. Vivian's not going to get in any trouble, though I gave her a stern talking to."

"You can be stern," Sadie teased. Will poured more wine into her glass, winking.

"It was by chance Mike died during the shootout. It made Ted furious, because that affected his bottom line. That's one of the reasons I think he acted so dumb directly afterwards. He talked shit about Mike right in front of you, and then you were investigating. He knew you were on to him from the beginning, even when we weren't looking at him at all. That's why he sent you the texts and that macabre box."

"And he attacked Cody?"

"We think it was Tiffany, but it doesn't really matter. They were co-conspirators. Cody knew Mike's secret too, and knew that Ted and Tiffany knew it, and he was going to tell you before he left town. Whoever hit him over the head also planted the ivermectin and vape materials in his trailer, locking it behind them. I wish Cody would've told me when we questioned him. We might've been able to wrap it up then, but he was so focused on getting out of town."

"Thankfully, he's going to be okay," Sadie said. Cody was out of the hospital and recovering in a hotel until he was ready to leave town for good this time. Sadie wished him well. "When did you find out about Mike being Mike and not Malcolm?"

"Almost right away," Will admitted. "He wasn't very good at hiding it. He just wasn't really close enough to anyone to be found out. All his documents were still in his real name. He just used the persona."

"And his money?"

"He won the lottery, like we thought. That's why he left Stanford. He invested it, but spent a lot, and ran out after the stagecoach. Not sure what his plan was from that point on. He'd been investigating different scams he could run to earn money. His Netflix watch history was all conman documentaries."

"Wild," Sadie said, shaking her head.

"We haven't found any marks, though. He'd only planned to scam. He never got the opportunity to do it."

"So, was he a bad guy?"

Will rubbed his chin. "I don't know. You know I see things black and white, but Mike is pretty gray."

"Hm." The waiter came by to pick up the empty mushroom plate. Their time was running out.

"We didn't catch the Shultzes being the bad operators because of poor police work. The research was done, just no one put it together that they owned what they owned. That's on us. I'm sorry that you suffered because of it. You're amazing for putting it together."

Sadie felt a warm feeling spread through her chest, and it wasn't just the wine. "A compliment, detective? I'm all warm and fuzzy."

Will was serious. "You put it all together, and you got yourself out of the situation. You would've run out into the alley, screamed for help, found it, and been free. You didn't need us."

"But the police department was there," Sadie reassured him.

"Because of Kendall. Because she has you in her find friends on her phone, realized no one at the bakery knew where you were, spied on your phone, which the Shultzes hadn't been smart enough to turn off before putting it in Ted's truck, then drove by and saw the Shultzes plotting in the alley, realized something was wrong, and called the police." Sadie knew that they'd found zip ties, a shovel, and a gun in Ted's truck. They'd come back to the condo with a plan to deal with her. She suppressed a shiver.

The waiter appeared with their dinners, placing them in front of them. Sadie leaned in to smell hers. Yum.

"Any more questions before you lift your fork?" Will asked. "We're closing the chapter now."

Sadie thought hard. It didn't make sense to her because she couldn't understand killing someone, but she didn't think there would ever be an explanation of the Shultzes behavior that she would understand. When someone was as detached from reality that they could believe what they believed, was it truly possible for a rational person to understand them? She was just glad they couldn't hurt anyone else anymore.

She reached for her fork and took a bite of the creamy risotto under her scallops.

"Perfect," Will said.

"Now, this is a date," Sadie said, winking at him.

And it was a very pleasant one. When they weren't talking about a case, Will and Sadie had a lot to talk about. He was definitely getting a second date. And maybe even a third.

They decided to skip dessert in favor of walking to the ice cream shop instead. Sadie excused herself to the restroom while Will took care of the bill.

While she was touching up her lipstick, her phone buzzed, and she pulled it out of her purse. A text from Kendall.

911! Get out of there!

Sadie frowned at the screen.

What do you mean? We're leaving in a minute.

Her phone rang. A...phone call from Kendall? Kendall hated talking on the phone. Shit, it must be a real 911. She answered it, worried.

"Moose! Go out the back door, okay?"

"Kendall, what are you talking about?"

"Uh...I just. I know you're at Elk & Olive because I saw it on the Find Friends—"

"That's only for emergencies. We talked about this."

"Yes, well, this is an emergency because I was walking by and I saw someone and I think you would like to go out the back when you leave."

"Who did you see? I can't think of anyone I don't want to see."

"I can think of one person," Kendall said, voice squeaking. "Shit, he saw me, I think."

"Are you running?" Sadie asked. She could hear footfalls slapping the sidewalk on the other side of the phone.

"Get out of there!" Kendall shouted. "For your own good!" The call disconnected. Sadie stared at it, then at herself in the mirror. What an odd interaction.

But when she walked back into the dining room, ready to regale Will with Kendall's latest antics, she saw why Kendall had told her to leave out the back. Standing at the front of the restaurant, waiting for a table, was a tall, broad shouldered, shaggy-haired blonde man. His beard was neatly trimmed, his suit flawlessly tailored. Sadie's heart beat fast. He was back.

Then she noticed the slim brunette on his arm. He was smiling into her eyes adoringly, and her stomach dropped.

"Everything okay?" Will asked from beside her. He had her sweater in hand, their table abandoned.

"Uh..."

He followed her line of sight and stiffened. He put his hand on her arm. Will knew that man. He'd once accused him of murder.

"Let's go out the back," Sadie said softly, turning away before the man spotted them.

"Okay," Will said, his hand at the small of her back. He looked over his shoulder once, but she grabbed his other hand and pulled him along. She wanted out of there immediately. She needed cool air on her face to think through what she'd just seen. The impossible thing she'd just seen.

Merritt West was back in town. And judging by the rock on that brunette's finger...he'd brought a fiancé with him.

* * *

Thank you for reading! As an independent author, it means the world to me. If you loved this book, please leave a review on Amazon, Goodreads, BookBub, or your favorite book site. Reviews help new readers find my books, and new readers means more books for all!

Sadie and the gang return next in Election Day Murder, coming to Amazon and Kindle Unlimited Winter 2023! Can't wait until then? Sign up for my newsletter at https://suepepper author.com/stay-in-touch/ to be the first to know when my next interstitial short story drops this fall!

Author's Note

When I write the settings in this series, sometimes they're completely made up (Bad Hair Day, the salon), sometimes they're inspired by real places (Slice Slice Baby, the pizzeria based on Pinky G's) and sometimes nothing I can fictionalize is as good as the actual place. This book contains one of those places, D.O.G., or Down on Glen. Listen to me. If you visit Jackson, you must go there in the morning and order the local burrito. Order it spicy if you like heat at all. While you wait at the window, gaze upon the stickers on the fridges. Do you have a cool sticker to offer? Offer it to the ski bum behind the counter. Then either eat the burrito there with a bottle of hot sauce nearby or take a to-go container of hot sauce and bike/walk/drive over to Snow King a few blocks away and park at the base of it and eat your burrito while you watch the skiers/hikers/dogs depending on the season. Do you feel that? You're having a unique Jackson Hole experience. One that I miss terribly. As is obvious by how hyper focused I am on it both in this book and in this Author's Note.

Anyway.

The Jackson Hole Shootout is real and is a 65-year tradition.

I saw it when I visited Jackson with my family in middle school, and it left a lasting impression on me. As far as I know, it is not this dramatic in real life. The Jackson Hole Playhouse does not have an attached large theater but does offer quality family-friendly dinner theater that's a darn good time. The Jackson Hole Rodeo is twice weekly from Memorial Day to Labor Day and is a great way to experience the tradition.

In January 2022, a Jackson childcare center was served a lease termination, leading to twenty-four families losing their care. The largest childcare center in Jackson went on record to say that they'd love to help, but their waitlist was already 200 plus families long. One of those was me, the article actually reminded me to go cancel my kids out since we'd moved away. The center ended up finding a new home, but that event inspired the mystery in this novel.

Jackson Hole is in the midst of a housing crisis. Many, many people, including my family, have been forced out of the community because of income inequality, a lack of affordable housing, and encroaching billionaires. I am donating a portion of the profits from this series to ShelterJH, an organization building grassroots and political power in Jackson Hole so that all community members can live where they work. I encourage you to give them your support and read through their policy platform. They have much better ideas on how to fix the problem than my works of fiction provide.

Acknowledgments

This is the most difficult project I've ever completed. There were days, weeks even, when I was sure I wouldn't complete it in time. Over the course of the drafting of this book, my dear father died, my beloved dog died, and I got a moderate-to-bad case of Covid while solo parenting two also-sick kids. It was the worst summer of my life, and after summer 2020, when I lost my mom after a long cancer battle mid-pandemic, that's really saying something.

All this to say, without the support and cheerleading of my friends and family, this book wouldn't have made it into your hands. Forgive me, this list is long and if your name is not on it, it's only because I'm writing this while my kids are destroying our house and I am very distracted.

Thank you, Whitney, always, for sending tacos and cheese-cake when you knew I would be too sad to eat, and for always being my person. I'm sorry we both had to go through this, but I'm so glad we had each other.

Thank you, Jen, for going way out of your way to get me my meds and check in with me. I'm so glad our kids are friends and soccer brought us together.

Thank you, Lea, for being the best beta reader on Earth, for loving these characters as much as I do, and for sending your sweet notes and cards when you know I need encouragement.

Thank you Rachael, Kristen, and Leah for you know what, and a particular thank you to Rachael for sending me a case of Dr Pepper after my dad died. Literally that was the best gift.

Thank you to my husband for taking care of us from afar while we were sick. We're glad you didn't get it to, though I'll be jealous of your sick-kid-free hotel time forever anyways.

Thank you, kiddos. I don't know that we'll ever dig out of the generalized mess that we made while isolating for ten days, but I'll remember the movies, the Legos, the activities, and the laughs that sustained us through the days forever.

Thank you family, from my sisters to my in-laws, for the love, support, and help with the kids.

Thank you to my advanced readers team. You help other readers discover my books, and I'm so grateful to you!

Thank you to the Late Night Writers Club on TikTok and Discord for the sprints and the encouragement, and as always thank you to my Sisters in Crime Guppies and Columbia River Chapters.

Lastly, thank you readers. This book was a month later than I'd planned, so thank you for your patience. I pinch myself because people I *don't know* are reading my books all the time, and while I'm sore, I'm grateful.

About the Author

Sue Pepper writes not so cozy mysteries in the Pacific Northwest where she lives with her two kids, elderly dachshund, and real life action hero husband. A former resident of Jackson Hole, Wyoming pushed out by the billionaire-caused housing crisis, she enjoys writing revenge and redemption for the fictional residents of her Jackson Hole Moose's Bakery Not So Cozy Mystery series, starting with her debut, Mountain Town Murder.

Find her online at www.suepepperauthor.com, Facebook, TikTok, and Instagram.

Also by Sue Pepper

Jackson Hole Moose's Bakery Not So Cozy Mystery Series

Available in print wherever books are sold, and in ebook form on Amazon and Kindle Unlimited:

Mountain Town Murder, #1

Hot Springs Murder, #2

Boss Babe Murder, #3

Tourist Trap Murder, #4

Election Day Murder, #5 - coming winter 2023!

FREE interstitial short stories available at www.suepepperauthor.com/books:

Escape From the North Pole, #1.5

A Deadly Secret Admirer, #2.5

A Patchwork of Peril, #3.5

Fall Interstitial, #4.5 - coming soon!